Scott The Piano Guy's™
Favorites and Holiday Songs Fake Book

Produced by

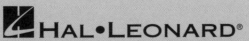

7777 W. BLUEMOUND RD. P.O. BOX 13819 MILWAUKEE, WI 53213

Visit Hal Leonard Online at
www.halleonard.com

contents

Some Notes From Scott ...

I hope you're as thrilled with this fake book as I was creating it! Through the feedback from thousands of television show viewers, plus the thousands of workshop attendees and online students many of whom were just starting down the path of non- classical piano playing, I was able to include all the things that everyone most wanted and needed in a fake book. I'm proud to say that I listened! It's all in this first-of-its-kind fake book.

Having said that, I need to explain a few things that I think will answer many of the questions you may have when you dig into playing your favorite tunes.

How to Use the Chord Charts

You'll immediately notice that at the beginning of every tune, there is a set of chord diagrams split into an upper and lower row. The upper row contains diagrams of the basic chords designated by the symbols used in the tune. Immediately below every basic chord is a possible chord substitution that you may want to try and use as you begin to get the tune "under hand." These more advanced chords are simply substitutions that professional players tend to use when they are really out working gigs. You will find that they will sound a little more polished, or perhaps jazzy (for lack of a better description). Understand that these more advanced substitutions are not cast in stone. There is no absolute right or wrong choice when choosing whether or not to play the basic or the more advanced chords. Let your ear and taste be your guide. Also, there will be times when the basic and advanced chords listed are exactly the same. That usually occurs where there is just no logical chord substitution to be made.

I think the chord diagrams are the best part of my fake book, because they will allow you to kind of "get into a real player's head" a bit and start to understand why even if you play basic chords perfectly as listed in a lead sheet, you still might not sound like players that you hear out working professionally. Professionals tend to use more hip-sounding chord substitutions for the basic chord symbols given in a lead sheet. Now you can start to get a handle on some of those substitutions. You'll find that similar chord substitutions occur over and over, which will allow you to start internalizing and allowing them to sneak into your playing very naturally.

One Substitute to Watch Out For!

I think you'll quickly notice that one chord substitution is made time and time again: using a major 7th chord instead of a regular old major chord (i.e. C becomes Cmaj7). It is a great substitution that sounds great most of the time but has one major issue to watch out for: If the melody note that is being emphasized when you play the chord happens to be the root of the chord, you probably shouldn't use the substitution. For example:

You have a C chord symbol given above a melody line that has E,F,G in that measure. Great! Go ahead and use the major 7th substitution and play a Cmaj7 instead of the regular C chord.

However, if you have a C chord symbol given above a melody line that has a single C note held through the measure - watch out! Because the C in the melody line is the root of.the C chord, it will tend to clash if you use the Cmaj7 as a substitute.

To give your ear a chance to hear this, just play any major 7th chord with your left hand while emphasizing the root note (the note the chord begins with) in your right hand in some octave above where you are playing the chord. It's pretty dissonant... So to be safe, just keep a look out for that "major 7th for a major" chord substitution when the melody line happens to be focusing on the root of the chord. You'll probably be happier just sticking to the original chord.

Voicings

Voicings is a term used for different variations of a chord that you can play that don't necessarily contain every note in the chord. Voicings give you the parts of a chord to leave out to make them simpler to play and still sound great. In most cases in the chord diagrams in this book, we have given you the entire chord in root position. It will be up to you to decide on using a voicing or not, depending on your taste and skill level. However, in a few cases (primarily 13th chords) we went ahead and gave you the chord diagram using a voicing when there was one very obvious one to use. Let me explain further...

You may have noticed that in the case of 9th chords, there are 5 notes. Playing all 5 of those notes is not only very difficult physically to finger, but can also sound a little "muddy." In the real world, players would seldom play all five notes in the 9th chord. Instead they would use a voicing to give them a simpler, cleaner-sounding version of the chord to play. For example, instead of playing all 5 notes in a C9 chord, which are C, E, G, B-flat, D I would probably choose to play just the E, B-flat, D in the chord (and maybe try to reach down and play the C root separately an octave lower).

This topic is more advanced than can be dealt with here in any depth, so I encourage you to find a book that deals with voicings to learn more. One tip I can give you is that the most important notes in a chord to play (which you need to know to be able to decide which ones to leave out) are the 3rd, 7th, and whatever else is in there that gives the chord its distinctive sound, like the 9th or 13th.

Slash Chords

(D/C, Fmaj7/G, Dm/E for example)

In lead sheet notation, slash chords direct you to play a particular note in the bass (in other words, the lowest note you hear). They work like this:

- Whatever the chord symbol is to the left of the slash is the actual chord you are supposed to play.

- Whatever the individual note name is to the right of the slash is the single note you are supposed to play in the bass.

For example, G/A means play a single A note down low in the bass (grab it with your sustain pedal to keep it sounding), and come up and play a G major chord in its normal position. In other words, play a G major chord over an A in the bass.

Am/C means play an A minor chord over a C in the bass. In this case the C is actually a note in the A minor chord. So another way you could look at it is that it is forcing you to play the A minor chord in an inversion with C on the bottom.

Know that sometimes the bass note is in the chord; sometimes it is not. You still just make sure that it is the lowest note you are playing.

For the slash chord in the chord diagrams of this fake book, we are showing you only the chord portion of the slash chord, not the bass note portion. Therefore it is your responsibility to get that bass note played even though it does not appear in the chord diagram.

Have fun!
Scott "The Piano Guy" Houston

ALL THE THINGS YOU ARE
from VERY WARM FOR MAY

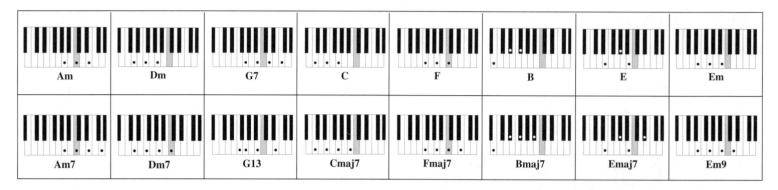

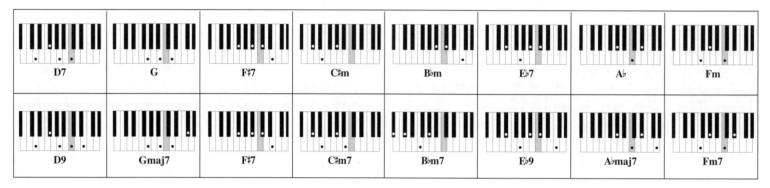

Lyrics by OSCAR HAMMERSTEIN II
Music by JEROME KERN

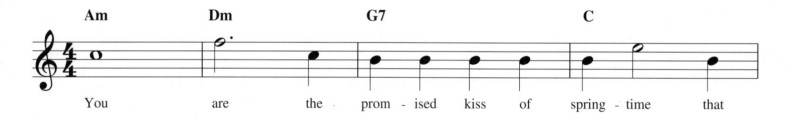

You are the prom-ised kiss of spring-time that

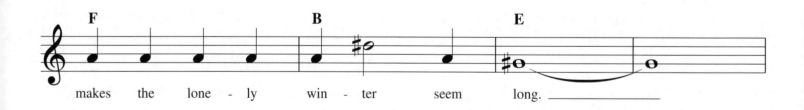

makes the lone-ly win-ter seem long. _____

You are the breath-less hush of eve-ning that

trem - bles on the brink of a love - ly song.

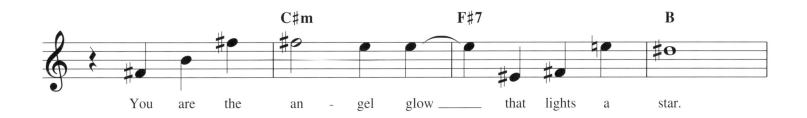

You are the an - gel glow _____ that lights a star.

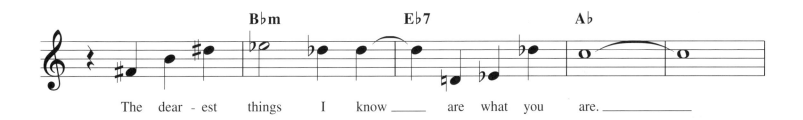

The dear - est things I know _____ are what you are. _____

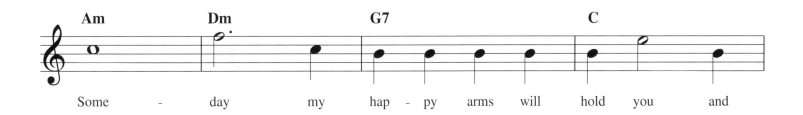

Some - day my hap - py arms will hold you and

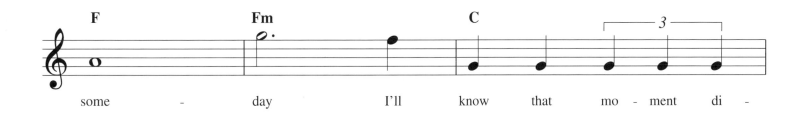

some - day I'll know that mo - ment di -

vine, when all the things you are are mine.

AMAZING GRACE

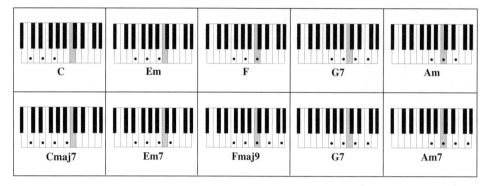

Words by JOHN NEWTON
From A Collection of Sacred Ballads
Traditional American Melody
From Carrell and Clayton's Virginia Harmony
Arranged by Edwin O. Excell

ANGELS WE HAVE HEARD ON HIGH

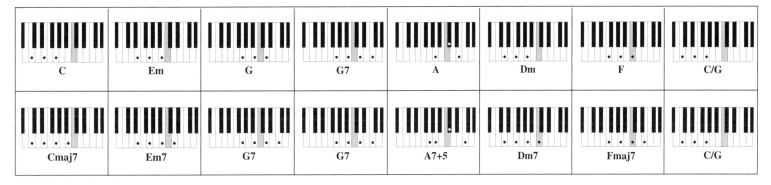

Traditional French Carol
Translated by JAMES CHADWICK

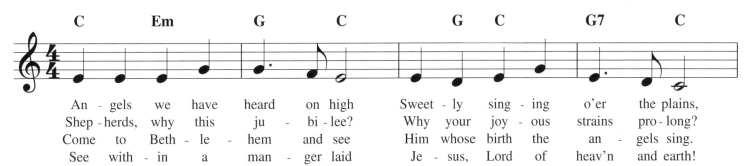

An - gels we have heard on high Sweet - ly sing - ing o'er the plains,
Shep - herds, why this ju - bi - lee? Why your joy - ous strains pro - long?
Come to Beth - le - hem and see Him whose birth the an - gels sing.
See with - in a man - ger laid Je - sus, Lord of heav'n and earth!

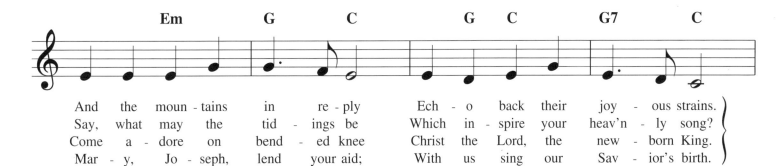

And the moun - tains in re - ply Ech - o back their joy - ous strains.
Say, what may the tid - ings be Which in - spire your heav'n - ly song?
Come a - dore on bend - ed knee Christ the Lord, the new - born King.
Mar - y, Jo - seph, lend your aid; With us sing our Sav - ior's birth.

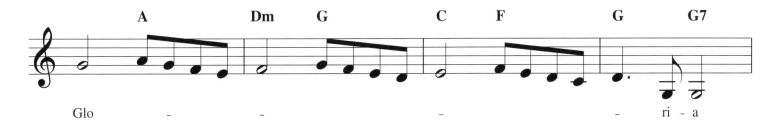

Glo - - - - ri - a

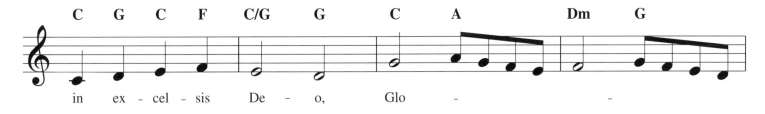

in ex - cel - sis De - o, Glo - -

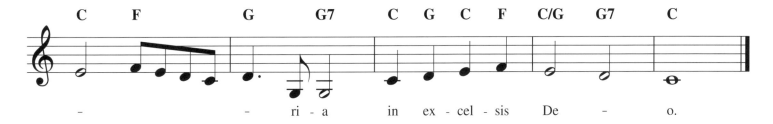

- - ri - a in ex - cel - sis De - o.

AUTUMN LEAVES

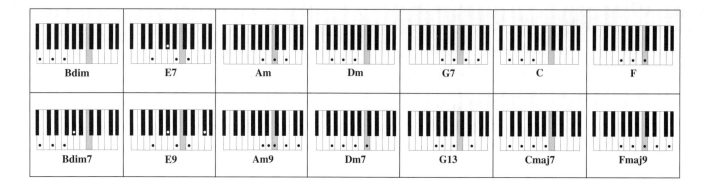

English lyric by JOHNNY MERCER
French lyric by JACQUES PREVERT
Music by JOSEPH KOSMA

The fall-ing

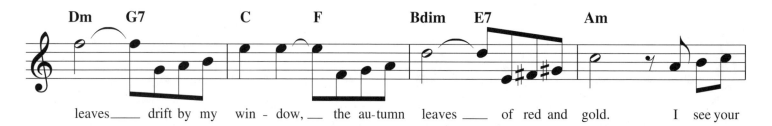

leaves___ drift by my win - dow, ___ the au-tumn leaves ___ of red and gold. I see your

lips, ___ the sum-mer kiss - es, ___ the sun-burned hands ___ I used to hold. Since you

went a - way ___ the days grow long, ___ and soon I'll hear ___ old win-ter's song. But I

miss you most of all my dar - ling, when au - tumn leaves start to fall.

BLUE SUEDE SHOES
from G.I. BLUES

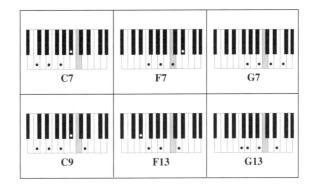

Words and Music by
CARL LEE PERKINS

Well it's one for the mon-ey, two for the show, three to get read-y now

go, cat, go but don't you step on my blue suede shoes.

You can do an-y-thing_ but lay off of my blue suede shoes.____

_____ Well you can knock me down,_ step on my face,_ slan-der my name all

o-ver the place._ Do an-y-thing that you want to do but uh-uh hon-ey, lay

off of my shoes._ Don't you step on my blue suede shoes.____

BLUEBERRY HILL

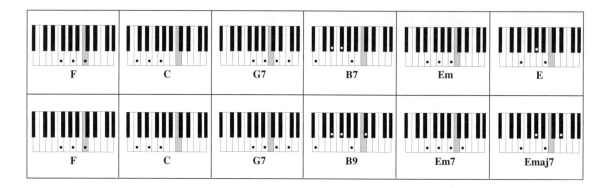

Words and Music by AL LEWIS,
LARRY STOCK and VINCENT ROSE

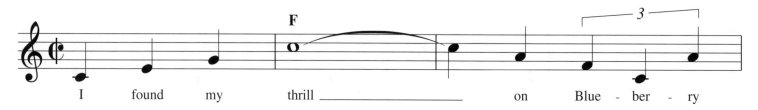

I found my thrill _____ on Blue - ber - ry

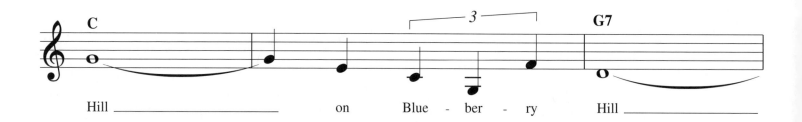

Hill _____ on Blue - ber - ry Hill _____

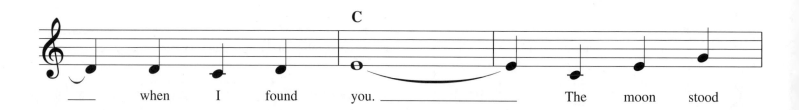

_____ when I found you. _____ The moon stood

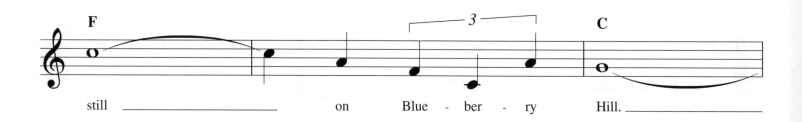

still _____ on Blue - ber - ry Hill. _____

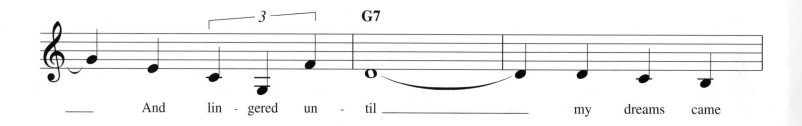

_____ And lin - gered un - til _____ my dreams came

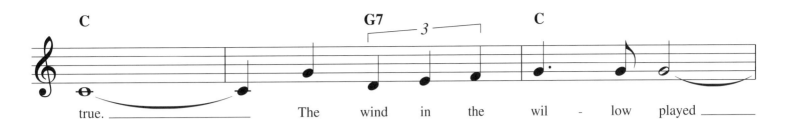

true. _____ The wind in the wil - low played _____

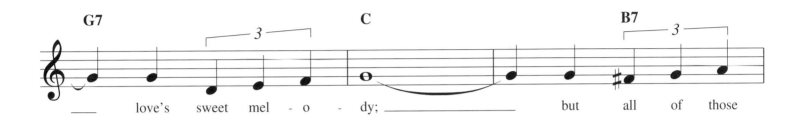

____ love's sweet mel - o - dy; _____ but all of those

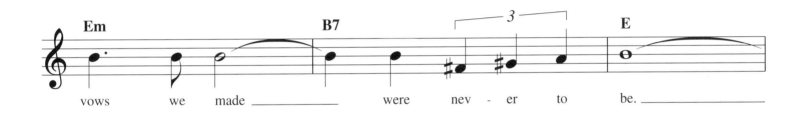

vows we made _____ were nev - er to be. _____

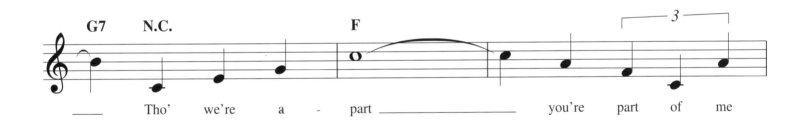

____ Tho' we're a - part _____ you're part of me

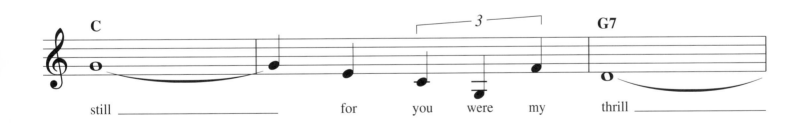

still _____ for you were my thrill _____

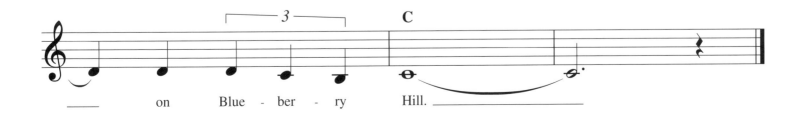

____ on Blue - ber - ry Hill. _____

BYE BYE BLACKBIRD
from PETE KELLY'S BLUES

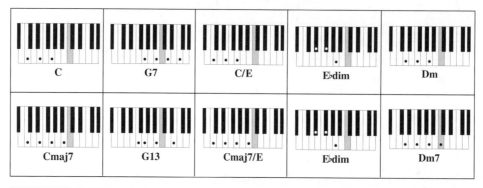

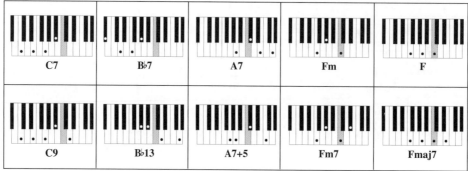

Lyric by MORT DIXON
Music by RAY HENDERSON

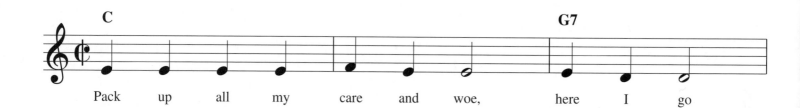

Pack up all my care and woe, here I go

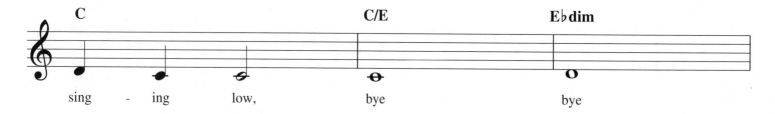

sing - ing low, bye bye

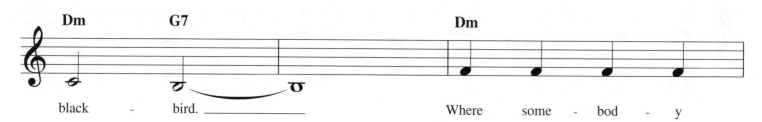

black - bird. _____ Where some - bod - y

waits for me, sug - ar's sweet, so is she,

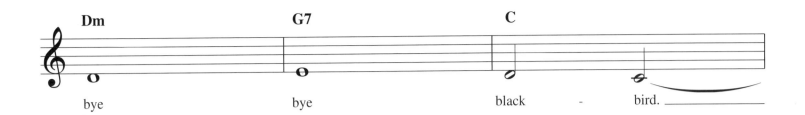

bye　　　　bye　　　black　-　bird.

No one here can love and un - der -

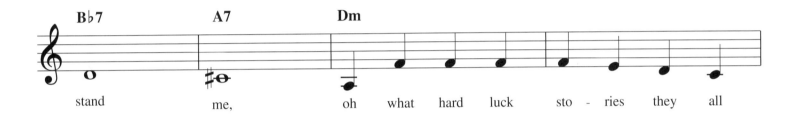

stand　me,　oh what hard luck sto - ries they all

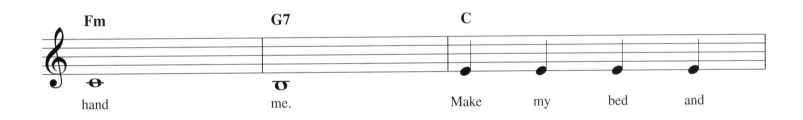

hand　me.　Make my bed and

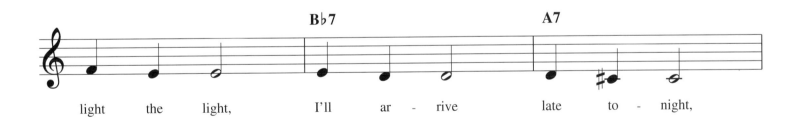

light the light, I'll ar - rive late to - night,

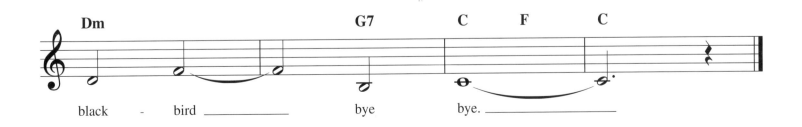

black - bird _____ bye bye. _____

CALL ME IRRESPONSIBLE
from the Paramount Picture PAPA'S DELICATE CONDITION

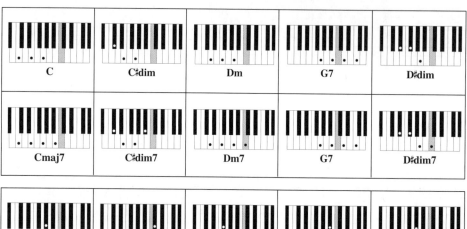

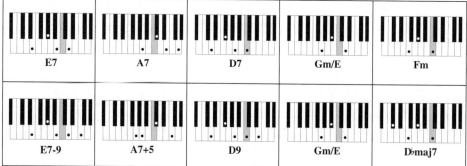

Words by SAMMY CAHN
Music by JAMES VAN HEUSEN

Call me ir - re - spon - si - ble, call me

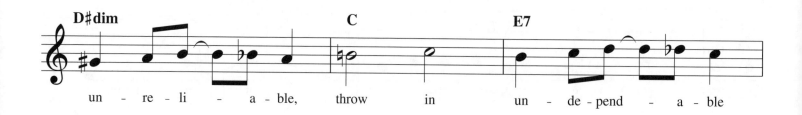

un - re - li - a - ble, throw in un - de - pend - a - ble

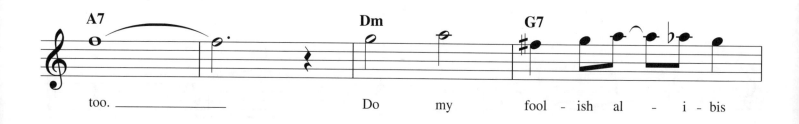

too. _____ Do my fool - ish al - i - bis

bore   you?   Well,   I'm   not too clev - er. I

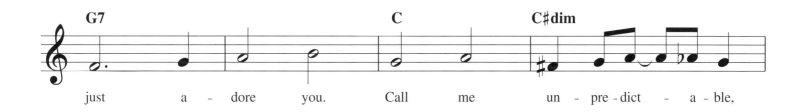

just   a - dore   you.   Call   me   un - pre -dict - a - ble,

tell   me   I'm im - prac - ti - cal, rain - bows

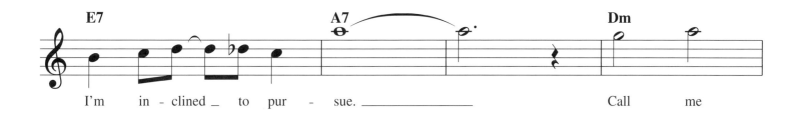

I'm in - clined _ to pur - sue. _____ Call me

ir - re - spon - si - ble, yes, I'm un - re - li - a - ble,

but it's un - de - ni - a - bly true, _____ I'm

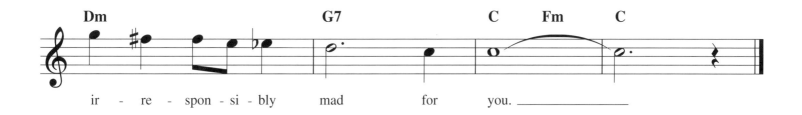

ir - re - spon - si - bly mad for you. _____

CAN YOU FEEL THE LOVE TONIGHT
from Walt Disney Picture's THE LION KING

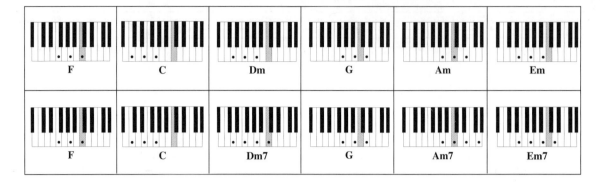

Music by ELTON JOHN
Lyrics by TIM RICE

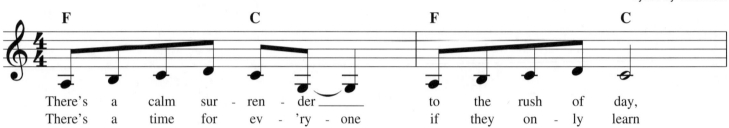

There's a calm sur-ren-der _____ to the rush of day,
There's a time for ev-'ry-one if they on-ly learn

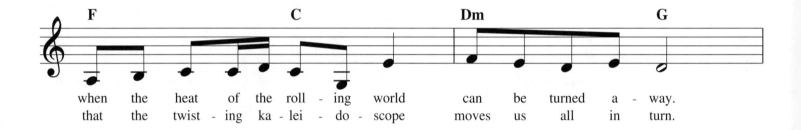

when the heat of the roll-ing world can be turned a-way.
that the twist-ing ka-lei-do-scope moves us all in turn.

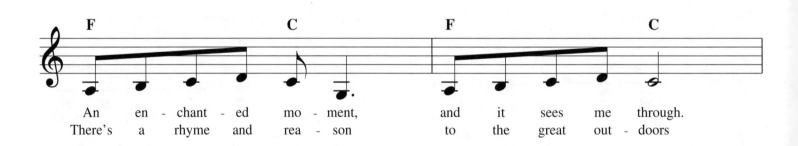

An en-chant-ed mo-ment, and it sees me through.
There's a rhyme and rea-son to the great out-doors

It's e-nough for this rest-less war-ri-or just to be with you. } And
when the heart of this star-crossed vo-ya-ger beats in time with yours.

can you feel the love to-night? It is where we are.

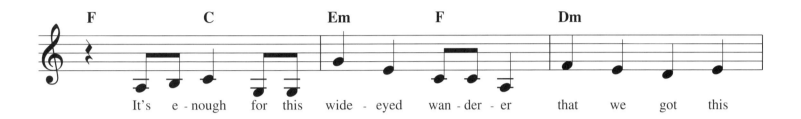

It's e-nough for this wide-eyed wan-der-er that we got this

far. And can you feel the love to-night,

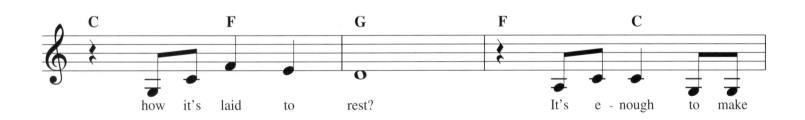

how it's laid to rest? It's e-nough to make

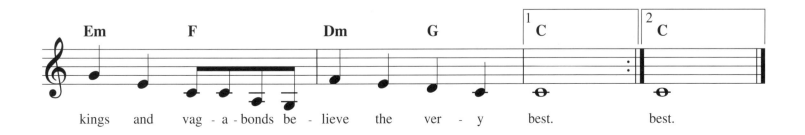

kings and vag-a-bonds be-lieve the ver-y best. best.

THE CHRISTMAS SONG
(Chestnuts Roasting on an Open Fire)

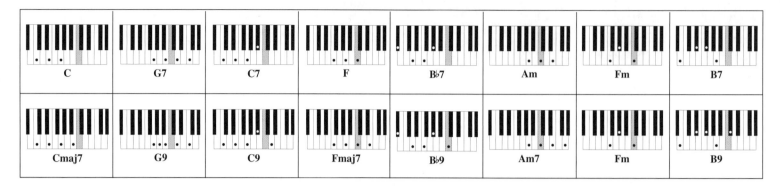

Music and Lyric by MEL TORMÉ
and ROBERT WELLS

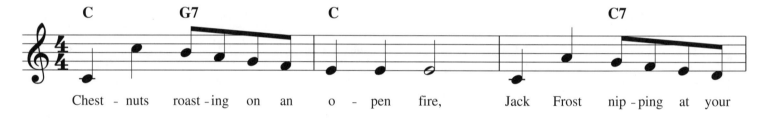

Chest - nuts roast -ing on an o - pen fire, Jack Frost nip -ping at your

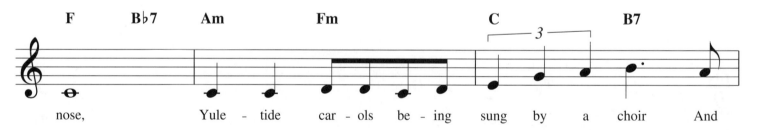

nose, Yule - tide car -ols be -ing sung by a choir And

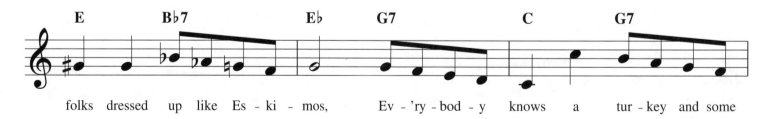

folks dressed up like Es - ki - mos, Ev - 'ry-bod - y knows a tur-key and some

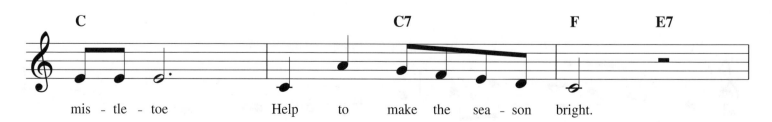

mis - tle -toe Help to make the sea - son bright.

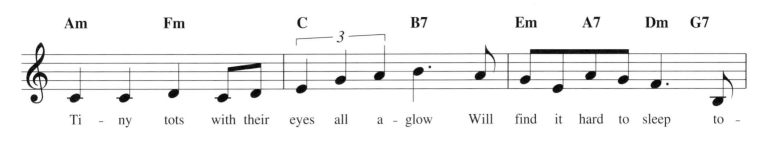

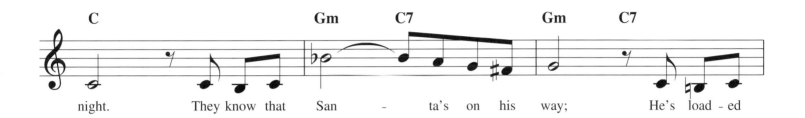

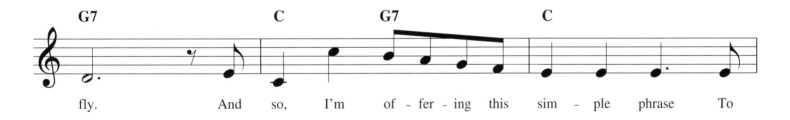

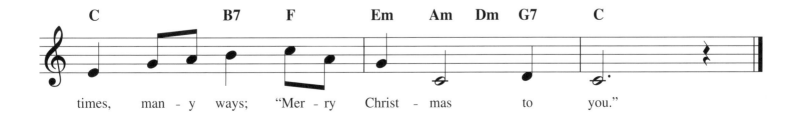

CRAZY

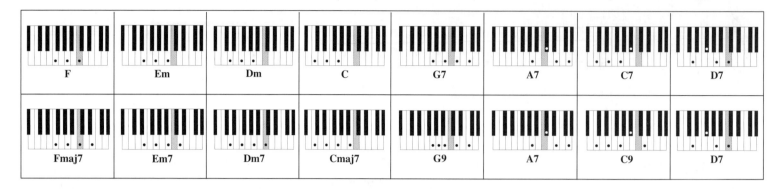

Words and Music by
WILLIE NELSON

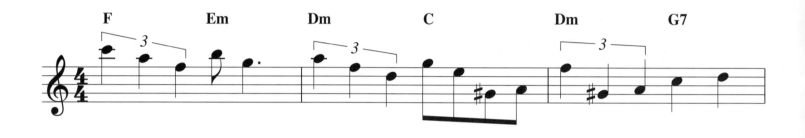

Cra - zy, _____ cra - zy for feel - in' so

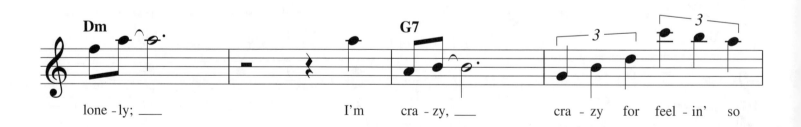

lone - ly; _____ I'm cra - zy, _____ cra - zy for feel - in' so

blue. I knew _____ you'd love me as long as you

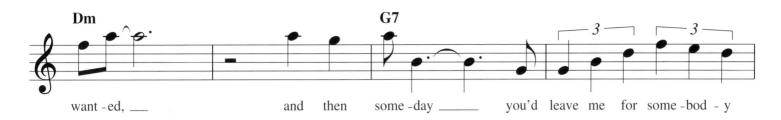

want -ed, ___   and then some -day _____ you'd leave me for some -bod - y

new.   Wor - ry _____ why do I let my - self

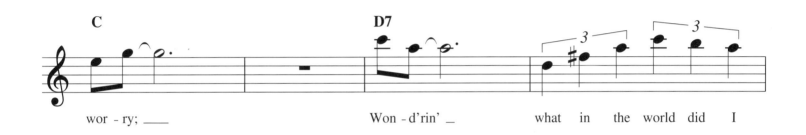

wor - ry; ___   Won -d'rin' _ what in the world did I

do.   Cra - zy _____ for think - ing that my love could

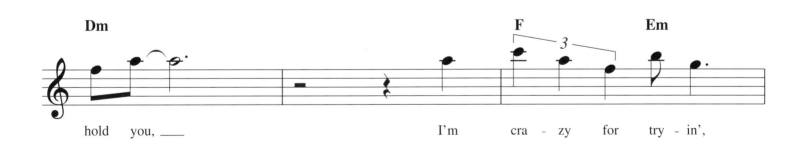

hold you, ___   I'm cra - zy for try - in',

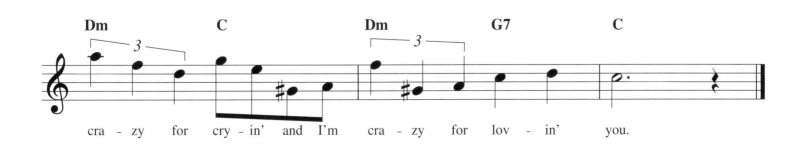

cra - zy for cry - in' and I'm cra - zy for lov - in' you.

DECK THE HALL

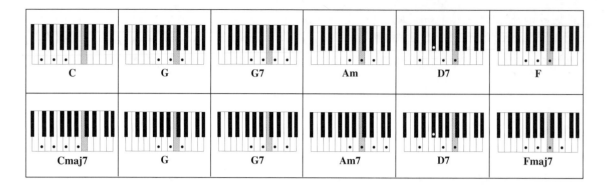

C G G7 Am D7 F

Cmaj7 G G7 Am7 D7 Fmaj7

Traditional Welsh Carol

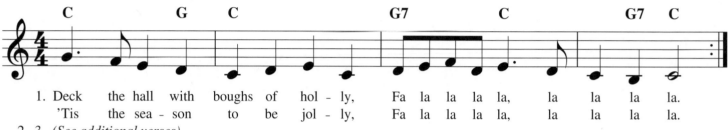

1. Deck the hall with boughs of hol - ly, Fa la la la la, la la la la.
'Tis the sea - son to be jol - ly, Fa la la la la, la la la la.

2., 3. *(See additional verses)*

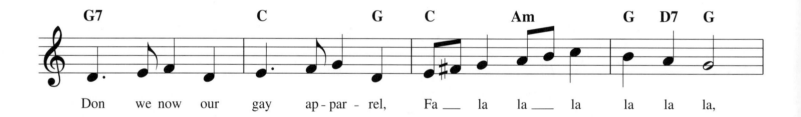

Don we now our gay ap - par - rel, Fa ___ la la ___ la la la la,

Troll the an - cient Yule - tide car - ol, Fa la la la la, la la la la.

Additional Verses

2. See the blazing Yule before us, Fa la la la la la, la la la la.
   Strike the harp and join the chorus, Fa la la la la la, la la la la.
   Follow me in merry measure, Fa la la la la la la la,
   While I tell of Yuletide treasure, Fa la la la la la, la la la la.

3. Fast away the old year passes, Fa la la la la la, la la la la.
   Hail the new, ye lads and lasses, Fa la la la la la, la la la la.
   Sing we joyous all together, Fa la la la la la la la,
   Heedless of the wind and weather, Fa la la la la la, la la la la.

ENDLESS LOVE

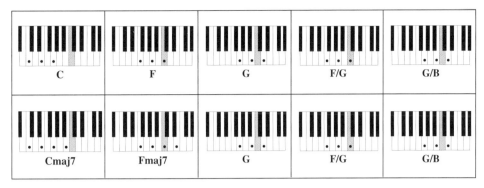

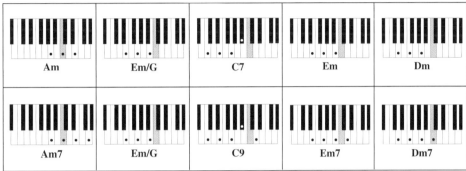

Words and Music by
LIONEL RICHIE

My love, ___ there's on - ly you in my life ___ the on - ly
Two hearts, _ two hearts that beat as ___ one ___ our lives have

thing that's right. ___ My first ___ love, _ you're ev - 'ry
just be - gun. ___ For - ev - er ____ I hold you

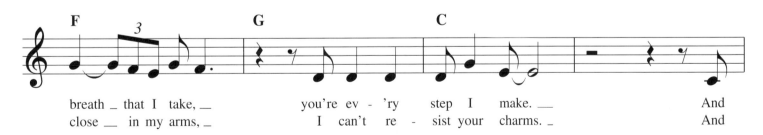

breath _ that I take, _ you're ev - 'ry step I make. ___ And
close _ in my arms, _ I can't re - sist your charms. _ And

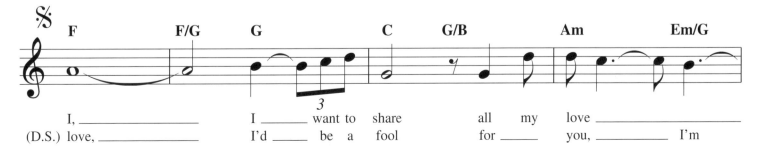

I, _____ I _____ want to share all my love _____
(D.S.) love, _____ I'd _____ be a fool for _____ you, _____ I'm

To Coda

with you; _____ no one else will do. _____ And your eyes, _
sure. you _ know I don't mind, _ 'cause

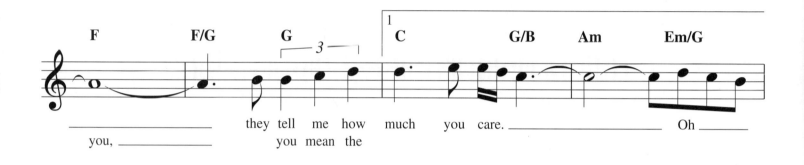

_____ they tell me how much you care. _____ Oh _____
you, _____ you mean the

yes, _ you will al - ways be _____ my end - less

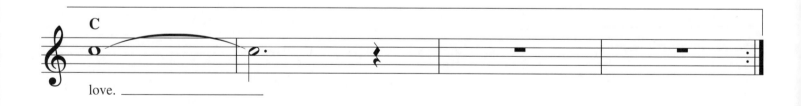

love. _____

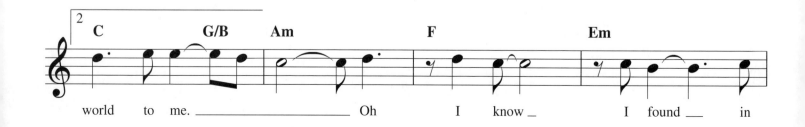

world to me. _____ Oh I know _ I found _ in

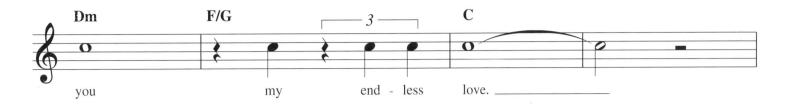

Dm **F/G** *3* **C**

you my end - less love. _____

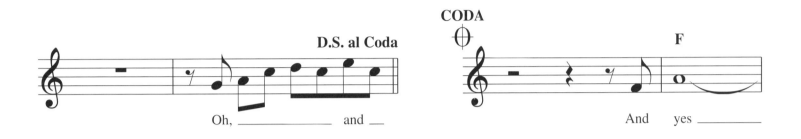

D.S. al Coda

Oh, _____ and __

CODA **F**

And yes _____

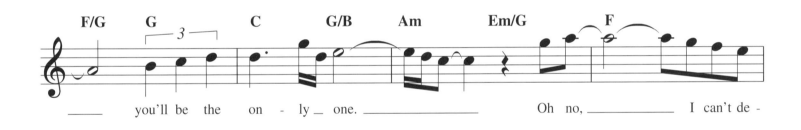

F/G **G** *3* **C** **G/B** **Am** **Em/G** **F**

_____ you'll be the on - ly _ one. _____ Oh no, _____ I can't de -

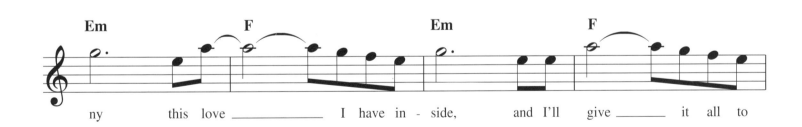

Em **F** **Em** **F**

ny this love _____ I have in - side, and I'll give _____ it all to

Em **Dm** **F/G** *3* **C**

you, my love, _____ my end - less love. _____

DO YOU HEAR WHAT I HEAR

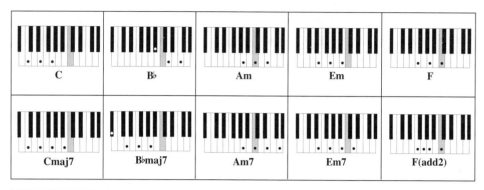

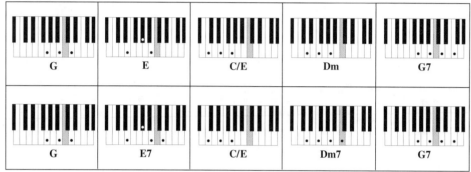

Words and Music by NOEL REGNEY
and GLORIA SHAYNE

Said the night wind to the lit - tle lamb,
lit - tle lamb to the shep - herd boy,
shep - herd boy to the might - y king,

Do you see what I see? _____ 'Way up in the sky, lit - tle
Do you hear what I hear? _____ Ring - ing through the sky, shep - herd
Do you know what I know? _____ In your pal - ace warm, might - y

lamb, Do you see what I see? _____ A
boy, Do you hear what I hear? _____ A
king, Do you know what I know? _____ A

star, a star, Danc - ing in the night, with a tail as big as a
song, a song, High a - bove the tree, with a voice as big as the
Child, a Child shiv - ers in the cold; Let us bring Him sil - ver and

DON'T GET AROUND MUCH ANYMORE

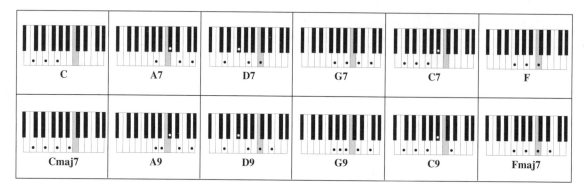

Words and Music by DUKE ELLINGTON
and BOB RUSSELL

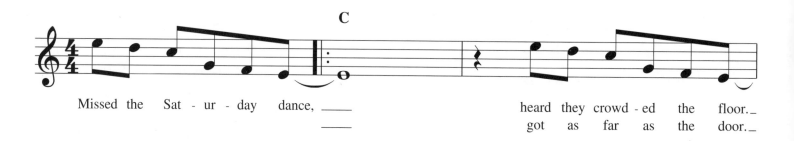

Missed the Sat-ur-day dance, _____ heard they crowd-ed the floor._
_____ got as far as the door._

_____ Could-n't bear it with-out you,
_____ They'd have asked me a-bout you,

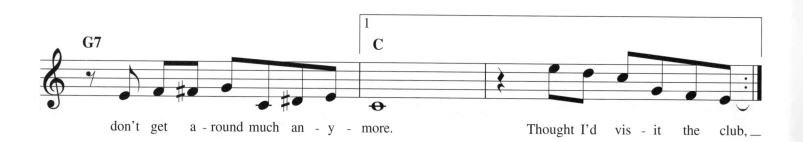

don't get a-round much an-y-more.   Thought I'd vis-it the club, _

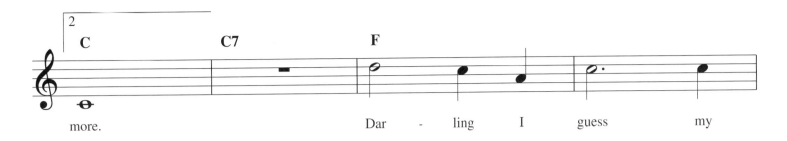

more.　　　Dar - ling I guess my

mind's more at ease.　But nev - er - the -

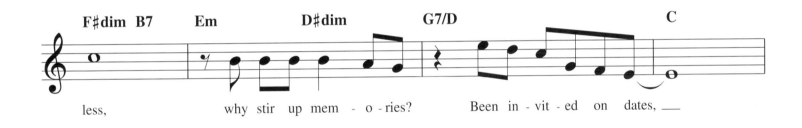

less,　why stir up mem - o - ries?　Been in - vit - ed on dates, ___

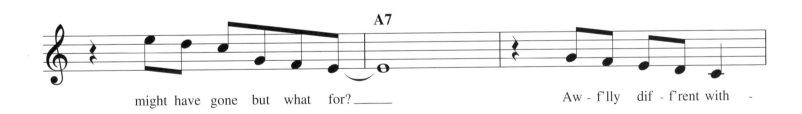

might have gone but what for? ___　Aw - f'lly dif - f'rent with -

out you,　don't get a - round much an - y - more. ___

DON'T KNOW MUCH

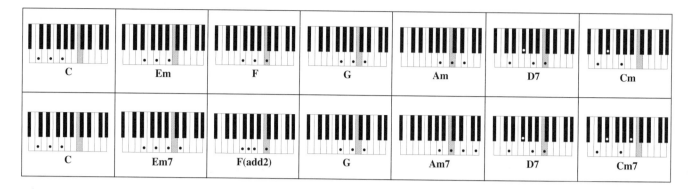

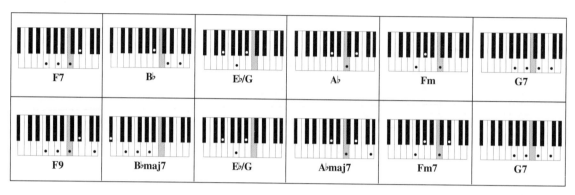

Words and Music by BARRY MANN,
CYNTHIA WEIL and TOM SNOW

Look at this face, I know the years are show - ing.
Look at these eyes, they've nev - er seen what mat - ters.
(D.C.) Look at this man, so blessed with in - spi - ra - tion.

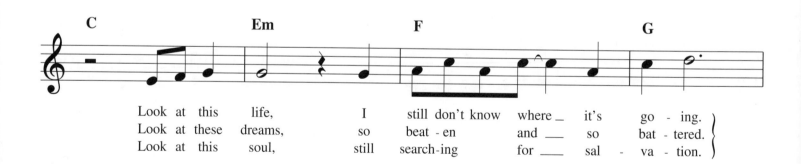

Look at this life, I still don't know where _ it's go - ing.
Look at these dreams, so beat - en and _ so bat - tered.
Look at this soul, still search - ing for _ sal - va - tion.

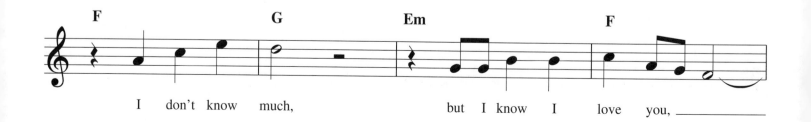

I don't know much, but I know I love you, _

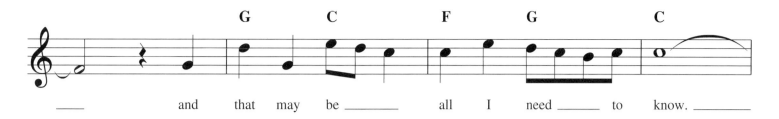

and that may be _____ all I need _____ to know. _____

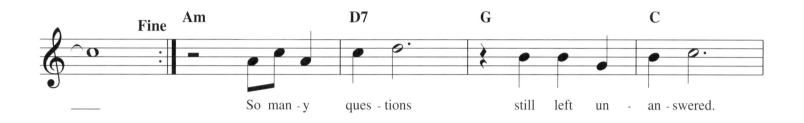

_____ So man - y ques - tions still left un - an - swered.

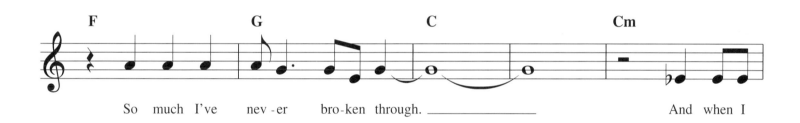

So much I've nev - er bro - ken through. _____ And when I

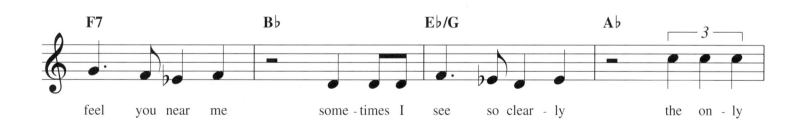

feel you near me some - times I see so clear - ly the on - ly

truth I've ev - er known is me and you. _____

THE FIRST NOEL

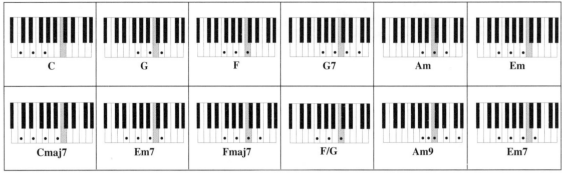

17th Century English Carol
Music from W. Sandy's *Christmas Carols*

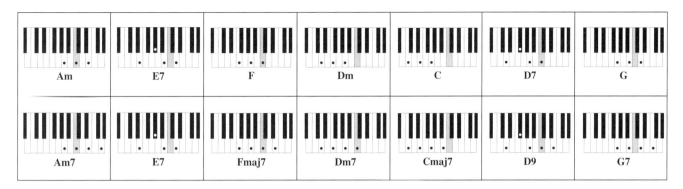

GOD REST YE MERRY, GENTLEMEN

19th Century English Carol

God rest ye mer - ry, gen - tle - men, Let noth - ing you dis - may, Re -
In Beth - le - hem, in Jew - ry, This bless - ed Babe was born, And
From God our Heav'n - ly Fa - ther, A bless - ed An - gel came; And

mem - ber Christ our Sav - iour Was born on Christ - mas Day, To
laid with - in a man - ger, Up - on this bless - ed morn; That
un - to cer - tain Shep - herds, Brought ti - dings of the same; How

save us all from Sa - tan's pow'r, When we were gone a -
which His Moth - er Mar - y, Did noth - ing take in
that in Beth - le - hem was born The Son of God by

stray;
scorn,   O _____ ti - dings of com - fort and joy, com - fort and
Name.

joy, O _____ ti - dings of com - fort and joy.

FLY ME TO THE MOON
(In Other Words)
featured in the Motion Picture ONCE AROUND

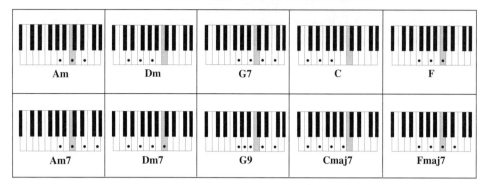

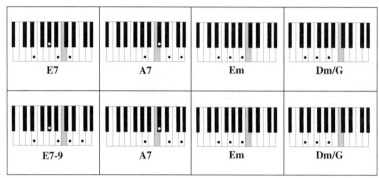

Words and Music by
BART HOWARD

Fly me to the moon, and let me play a - mong the stars; let me see what spring is like on Ju - pi - ter and Mars. In oth - er words, _____ hold my hand! _____ In oth - er words, _____ dar - ling kiss me! _____

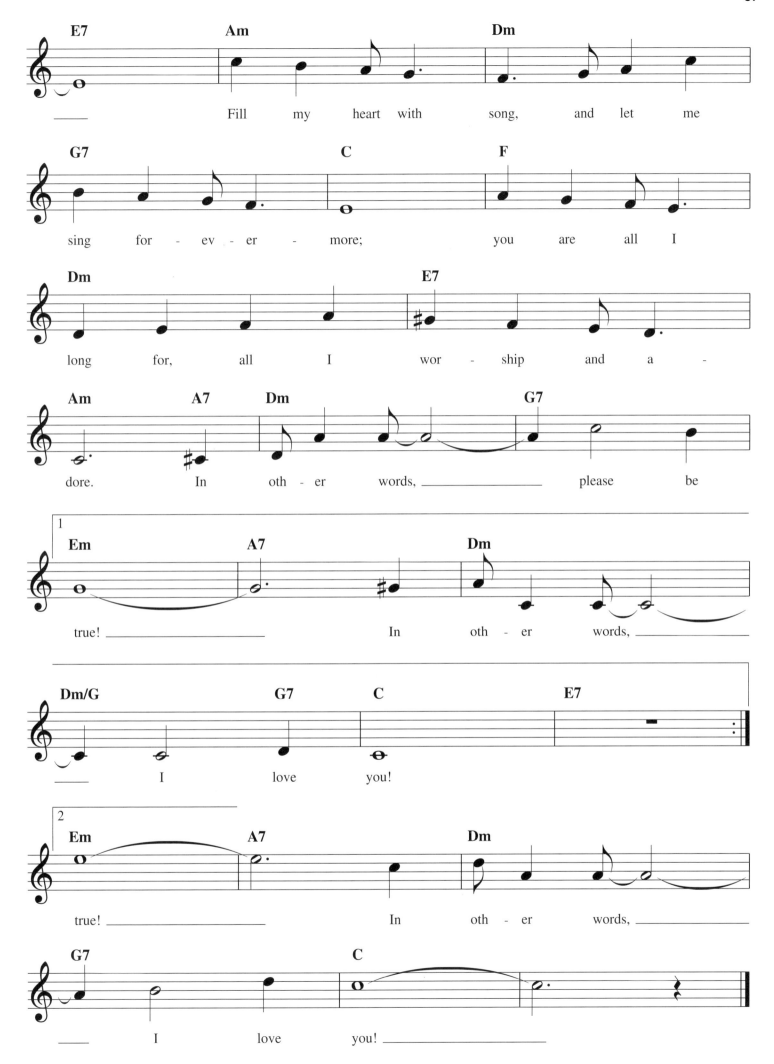

FROSTY THE SNOW MAN

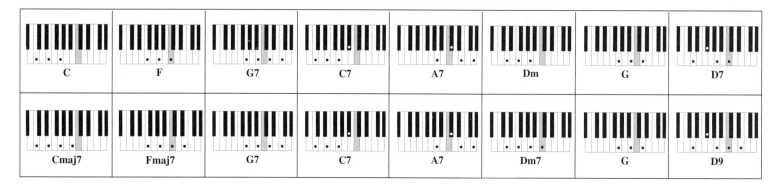

Words and Music by STEVE NELSON
and JACK ROLLINS

Fros - ty the snow man was a jol - ly hap - py soul, _
Fros - ty the snow man knew the sun was hot that day, _

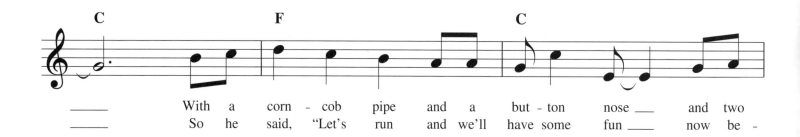

_____ With a corn - cob pipe and a but - ton nose ___ and two
_____ So he said, "Let's run and we'll have some fun ___ now be -

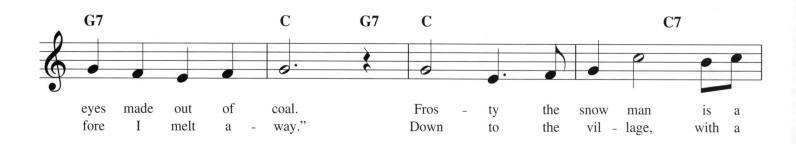

eyes made out of coal. Fros - ty the snow man is a
fore I melt a - way." Down to the vil - lage, with a

fair - y tale, they say, _____ He was made of snow but the
broom - stick in his hand, _____ Run - ning here and there all a -

GEORGIA ON MY MIND

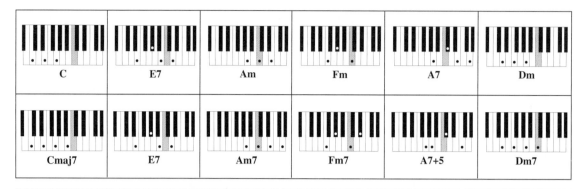

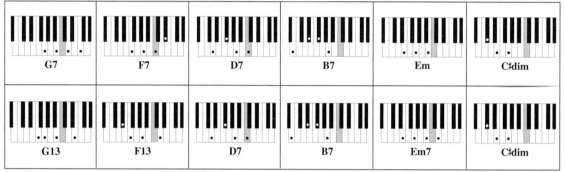

Words by STUART GORRELL
Music by HOAGY CARMICHAEL

C / E7 / Am

Geor - gia, _____ Geor - gia, _____ the whole day
Geor - gia, _____ Geor - gia, _____ a song of

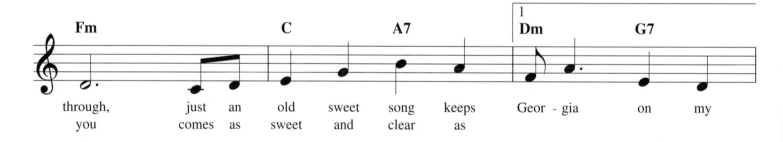

Fm / C / A7 / Dm / G7

through, just an old sweet song keeps Geor - gia on my
you comes as sweet and clear as

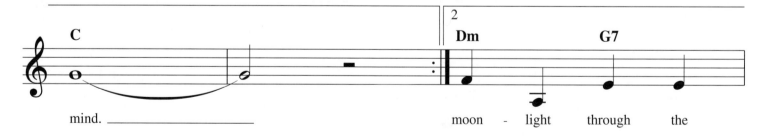

C / Dm / G7

mind. _____
moon - light through the

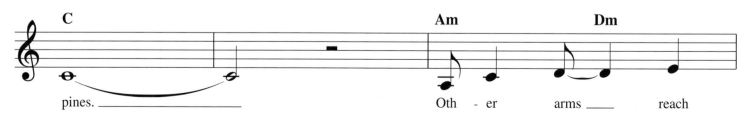

C / Am / Dm

pines. _____
Oth - er arms _____ reach

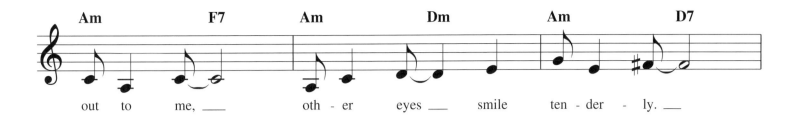

out to me, ___ oth - er eyes ___ smile ten - der - ly. ___

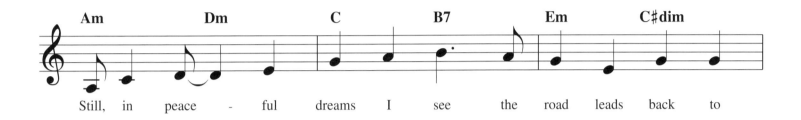

Still, in peace - ful dreams I see the road leads back to

you. _____ Geor - gia, ____ Geor - gia, ____

no peace I find. Just an old sweet song keeps

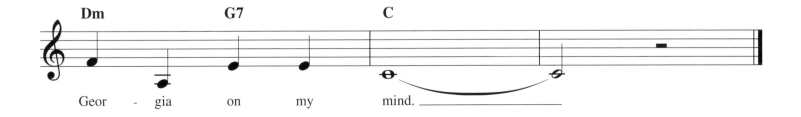

Geor - gia on my mind. _____

THE GIRL FROM IPANEMA
(Garôta de Ipanema)

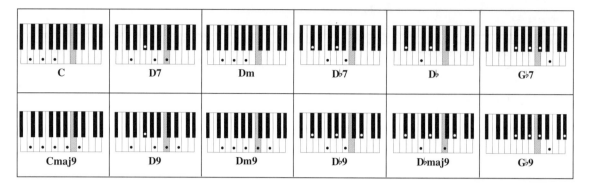

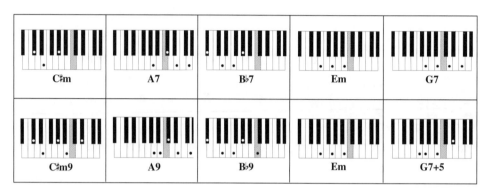

Music by ANTONIO CARLOS JOBIM
English Words by NORMAN GIMBEL
Original Words by VINICIUS DE MORAES

Tall   and   tan   and   young   and   love - ly,   the   girl   from   I   pa - ne -
When   she   walks   she's   like   a   sam - ba   that   swings   so   cool   and   sways _

- ma   goes   walk - ing,   and   when   she   pass - es,   each   one   she   pass - es   goes
_____   so   gen - tle,   that   when   she   pass - es,   each   one   she   pass - es   goes

"a - a - h!" _____   "a - a - h!" _____

Oh, _____   but   I   watch   her   so   sad - ly. _____

GOD BLESS' THE CHILD

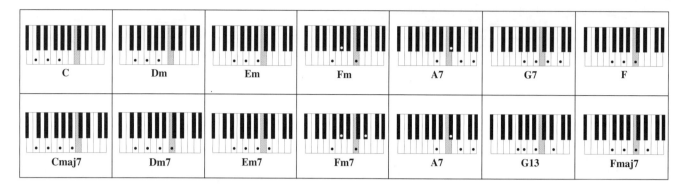

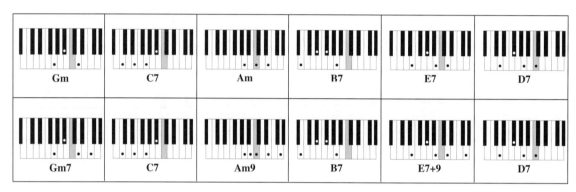

Words and Music by ARTHUR HERZOG JR.
and BILLIE HOLIDAY

Them that's got shall get, them that's
strong gets more, while the

not shall lose, so the Bi – ble said, and it still is news;
weak ones fade, emp – ty pock – ets don't ev – er make the grade;

Ma – ma may have, Pa – pa may have, but God bless' the child that's

45

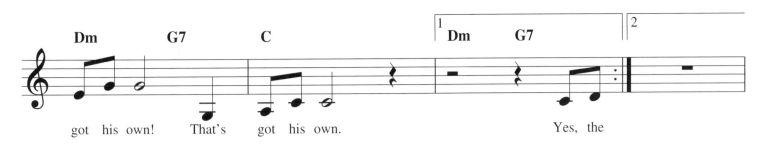

got his own! That's got his own. Yes, the

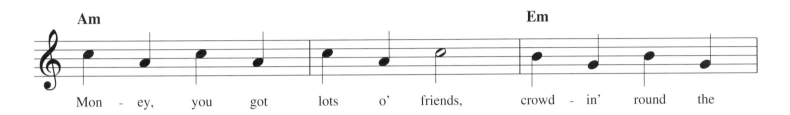

Mon - ey, you got lots o' friends, crowd - in' round the

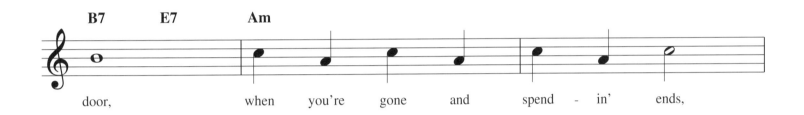

door, when you're gone and spend - in' ends,

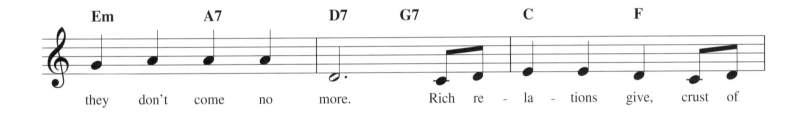

they don't come no more. Rich re - la - tions give, crust of

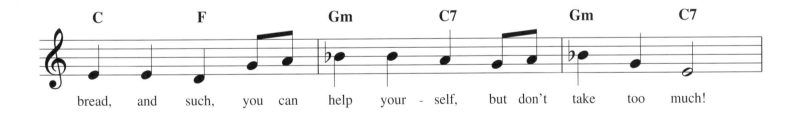

bread, and such, you can help your - self, but don't take too much!

Ma - ma may have, Pa - pa may have, but God bless' the child that's

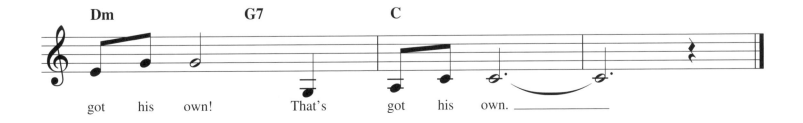

got his own! That's got his own. _____

GOOD KING WENCESLAS

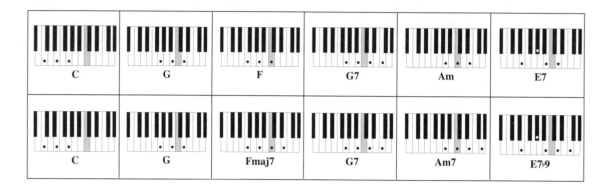

Words by JOHN M. NEALE
Music from *Piae Cantiones*

1. Good King Wen - ces - las looked out On the feast of Ste - phen,
2. "Hith - er, page, and stand by me, If thou know'st it, tell - ing,
3.-5. *(See additional verses)*

When the snow lay 'round a - bout, Deep, and crisp, and e - ven;
Yon - der pea - sant, who is he? Where and what his dwell - ing?"

Bright - ly shone the moon that night, Though the frost was cru - el,
'Sire, he lives a good league hence, Un - der - neath the moun - tain,

When a poor man came in sight, Gath - 'ring win - ter fu - el.
Right a - gainst the for - est fence, By Saint Ag - nes' foun - tain.'

Additional Verses

3. 'Bring me flesh, and bring me wine,
Bring me pine-logs hither:
Thou and I will see him dine,
When we bear them thither.'
Page and monarch, forth they went,
Forth they went together;
Through the rude wind's wild lament
And the bitter weather.

4. 'Sire, the night is darker now,
And the wind blows stronger;
Fails my heart, I know not how;
I can go no longer.'
'Mark my footsteps, good my page;
Tread thou in them boldly:
Thou shalt find the winter's rage
Freeze thy blood less coldly.'

5. In his master's steps he trod,
Where the snow lay dinted;
Heat was in the very sod
Which the saint had printed.
Therefore, Christian men, be sure,
Wealth or rank possessing,
Ye who now will bless the poor,
Shall yourselves find blessing.

HARK! THE HERALD ANGELS SING

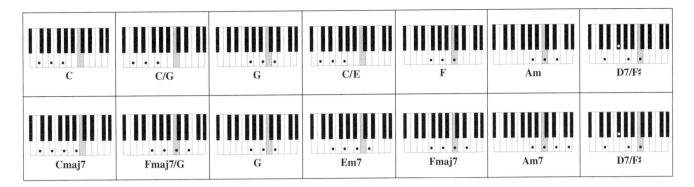

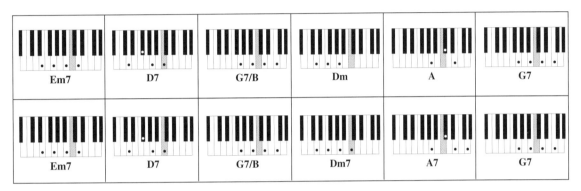

Words by CHARLES WESLEY
Altered by GEORGE WHITEFIELD
Music by FELIX MENDELSSOHN-BARTHOLDY
Arranged by WILLIAM H. CUMMINGS

GREAT BALLS OF FIRE

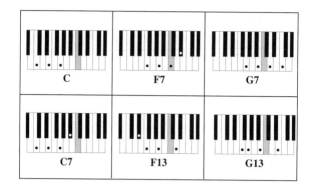

Words and Music by OTIS BLACKWELL
and JACK HAMMER

You shake my nerves   and you

rat - tle my brain. _   Too much   love   drives a   man   in - sane. _

You broke my will,   but what a thrill.   Good - ness   gra - cious, great _

_____ balls   of fire!   I laughed at   love   'cause I   thought it   was   fun - ny.

You came a - long and you moved _ me, hon - ey.   I changed my mind,

love's just fine. ___ Good - ness gra - cious, great ___ balls of fire!

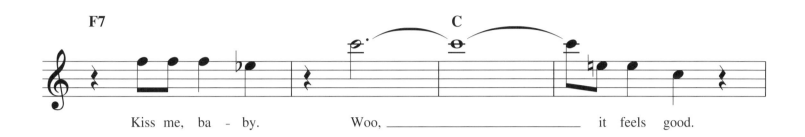

Kiss me, ba - by. Woo, _____ it feels good.

Hold me ba - by. { Girl, just let me love you like a lov - er should. ___ }
{ I want to love you like a lov - er should. ___ }

You're fine, ___ so kind. ___ I'm gon - na tell the world that you're

mine, mine, mine, mine. ___ I chew my nails and I twid - dle my thumb. ___

I'm real ner - vous but it sure is fun. ___ Come on, ba - by, you're

driv - ing me cra - zy. Good - ness gra - cious, great ___ balls of fire!

HEART AND SOUL
from the Paramount Short Subject A SONG IS BORN

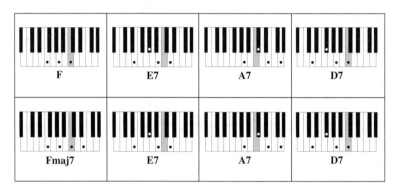

Words by FRANK LOESSER
Music by HOAGY CARMICHAEL

HERE, THERE AND EVERYWHERE

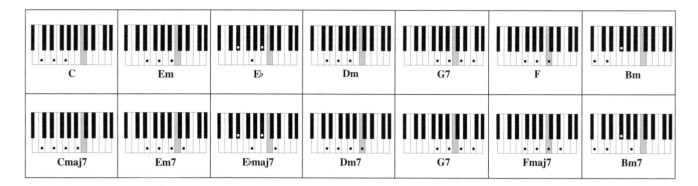

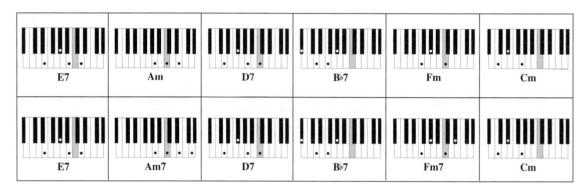

Words and Music by JOHN LENNON
and PAUL McCARTNEY

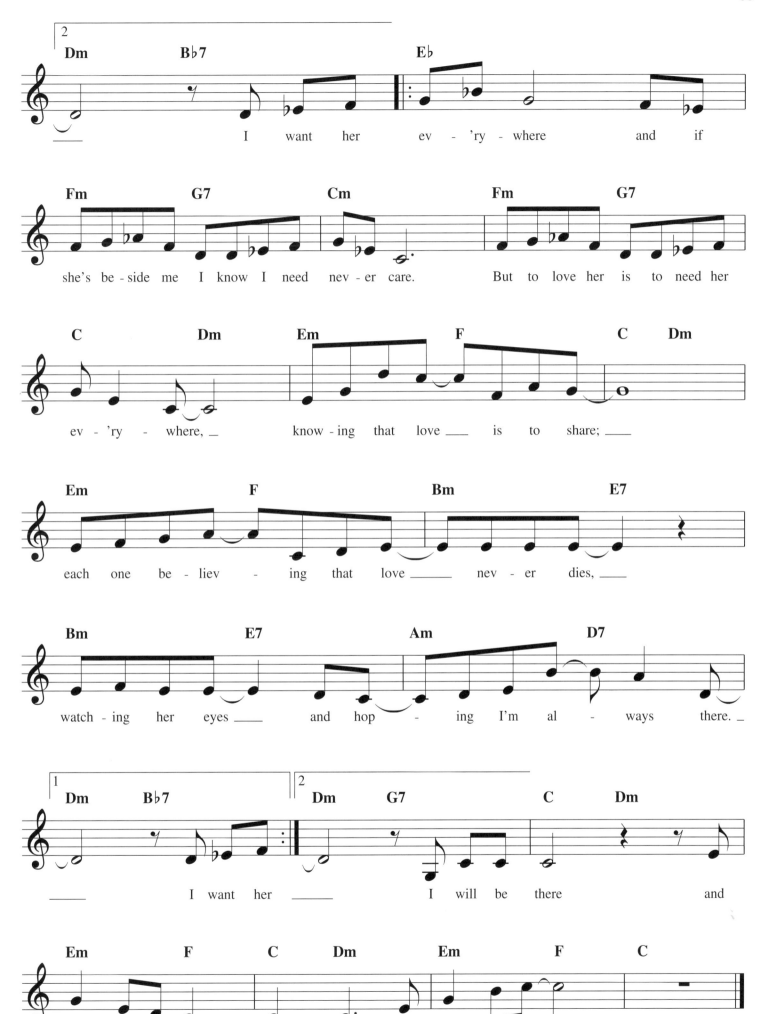

HEY JUDE

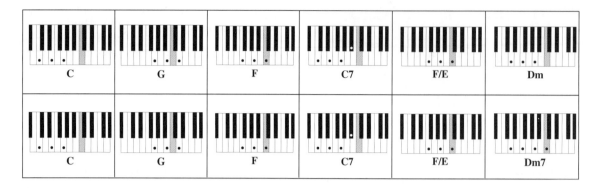

Words and Music by JOHN LENNON
and PAUL McCARTNEY

Hey Jude, _____ don't make it bad. Take a
sad song _____ and make it bet - ter. _____ Re -
mem - ber to let her in - to your heart. Then you can start ___
_____ to make it bet - ter. (Hey)

Jude, _____ don't be a - fraid. You were made to _____ go out and
Jude, _____ don't let me down. You have found her, _____ now go and

A HOLLY JOLLY CHRISTMAS

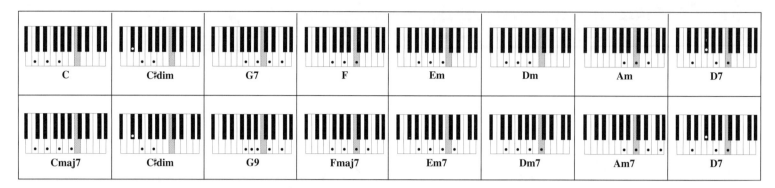

Music and Lyrics by
JOHNNY MARKS

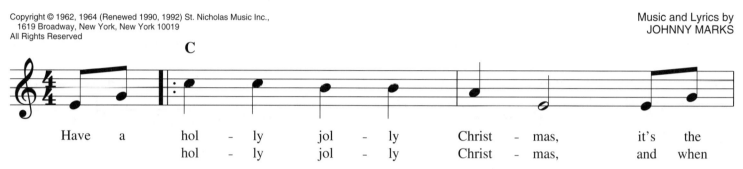

Have a hol - ly jol - ly Christ - mas, it's the
hol - ly jol - ly Christ - mas, and when

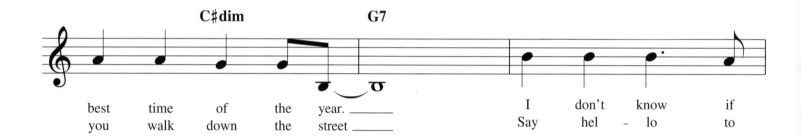

best time of the year. _____ I don't know if
you walk down the street _____ Say hel - lo to

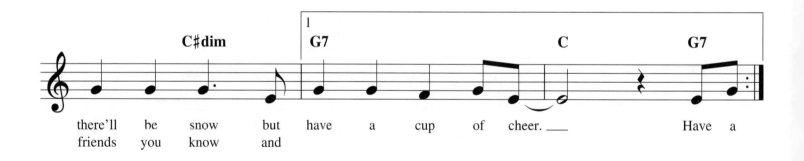

there'll be snow but have a cup of cheer. _____ Have a
friends you know and

ev - 'ry - one you meet.

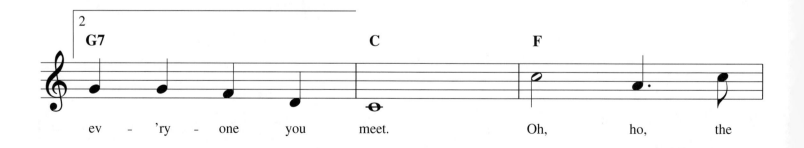

ev - 'ry - one you meet. Oh, ho, the

mis – tle – toe hung where you can see.

Some – bod – y waits for you, kiss her once for

me. Have a hol – ly jol – ly Christ – mas, and in

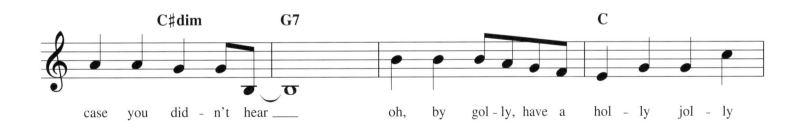

case you did – n't hear ____ oh, by gol – ly, have a hol – ly jol – ly

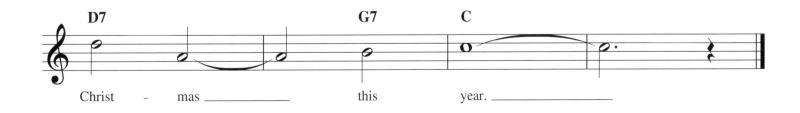

Christ – mas _____ this year. _____

HOUND DOG

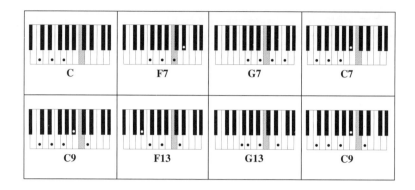

Words and Music by JERRY LEIBER
and MIKE STOLLER

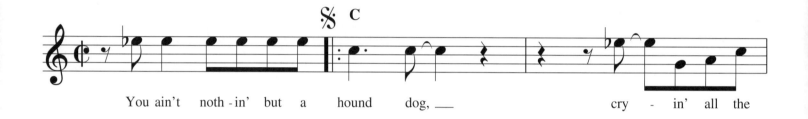

You ain't noth-in' but a hound dog, ___ cry - in' all the

time. You ain't noth-in' but a hound dog, ___

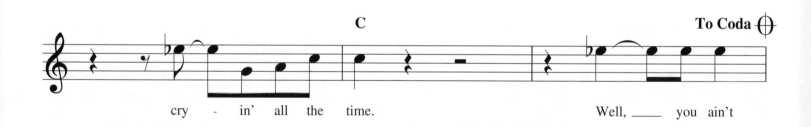

cry - in' all the time. Well, ___ you ain't

nev - er caught a rab - bit and you ain't no friend of mine. ___

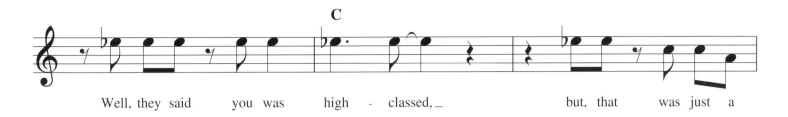

Well, they said you was high - classed, __ but, that was just a

lie. Yeah, they said you was high - classed, __

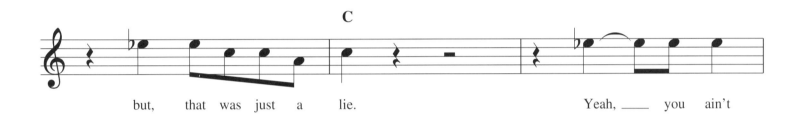

but, that was just a lie. Yeah, ___ you ain't

nev - er caught a rab - bit and you ain't no friend of mine. ___

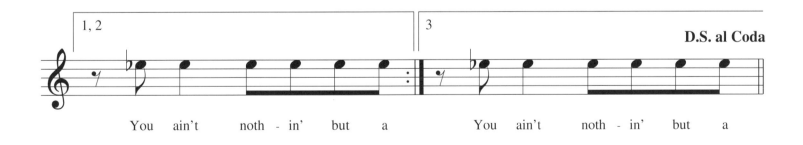

You ain't noth - in' but a   You ain't noth - in' but a

nev - er caught a rab - bit, and you ain't no friend of mine. ___

HOW SWEET IT IS
(To Be Loved by You)

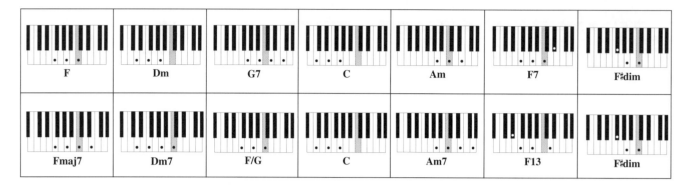

Words and Music by EDWARD HOLLAND,
LAMONT DOZIER and BRIAN HOLLAND

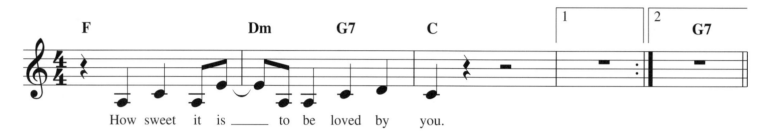

How sweet it is _____ to be loved by you.

I need-ed the shel-ter of some-one's arms;_
I close my eyes at night
(Instrumental)
won-der-ing where would I be with-out

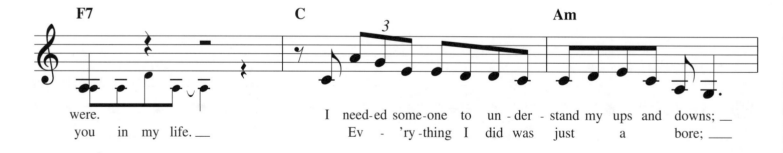

were.
you in my life. ____
I need-ed some-one to un-der-stand my ups and downs; __
Ev - 'ry-thing I did was just a bore; ___

ev - 'ry-where I went, seems I'd been there be-fore.
End Instrumental You were bet-ter to me than I
there you were ____ with sweet love and de-
But you bright - en up for me

vo - tion   deep - ly touch-ing my   e - mo - tion. ___
all   of   my   days ___   with   a   love so sweet in   so man - y   ways. ___ } I want to
was   to   my - self; ___   for   me   there's   you and there ain't   no - bod - y   else. ___ }

stop   and thank you,   ba - by;   I   want ___ to   stop   and thank you,

ba - by.   How   sweet   it   is _____ to   be   loved   by   you.

How   sweet   it   is _____ to   be   loved   by   you.

How   sweet   it   is _____ to   be   loved   by   you.

I LEFT MY HEART IN SAN FRANCISCO

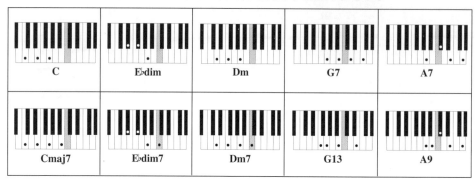

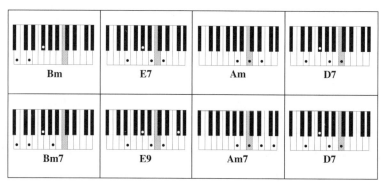

Words by DOUGLASS CROSS
Music by GEORGE CORY

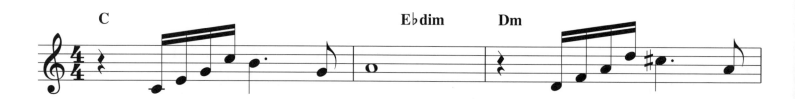

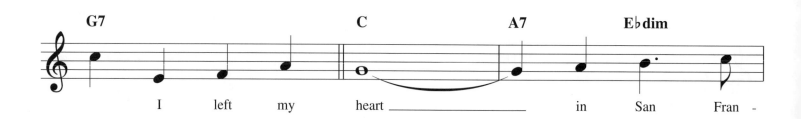

I left my heart _____ in San Fran -

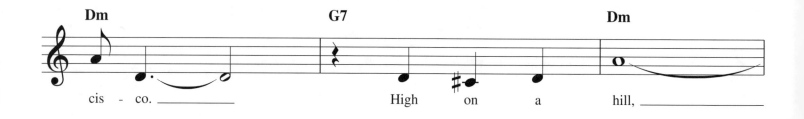

cis - co. _____ High on a hill, _____

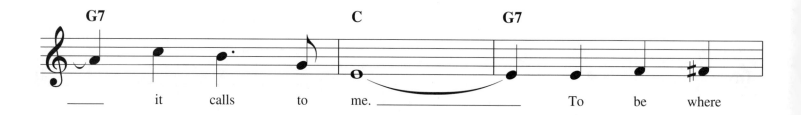

_____ it calls to me. _____ To be where

lit - tle ca - ble cars _____ climb half - way to the stars _____

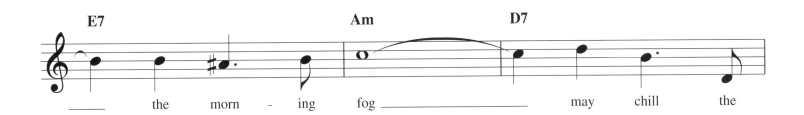

_____ the morn - ing fog _____ may chill the

air I don't care! My love waits there _____

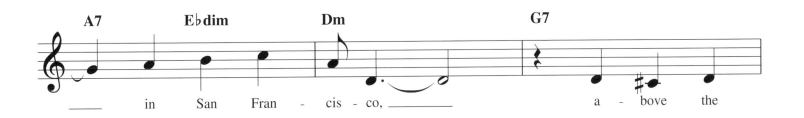

_____ in San Fran - cis - co, _____ a - bove the

blue _____ and wind - y sea. _____ When I come

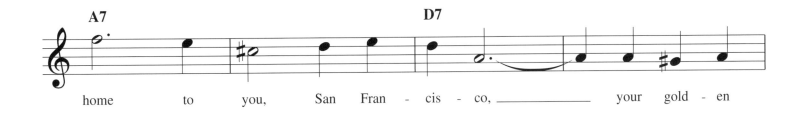

home to you, San Fran - cis - co, _____ your gold - en

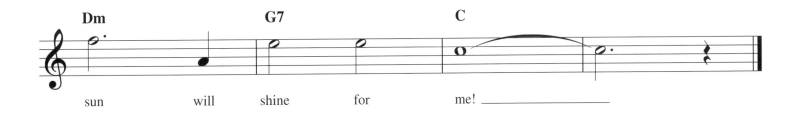

sun will shine for me! _____

I'LL BE HOME FOR CHRISTMAS

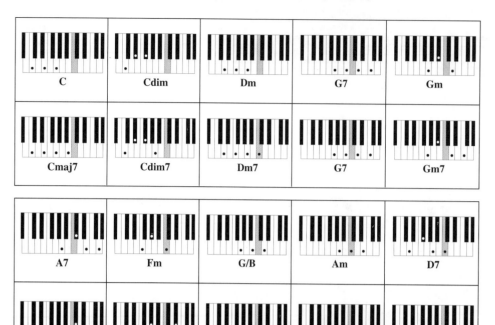

Words and Music by KIM GANNON
and WALTER KENT

I WILL REMEMBER YOU
Theme from THE BROTHERS McMULLEN

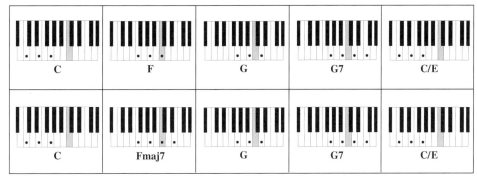

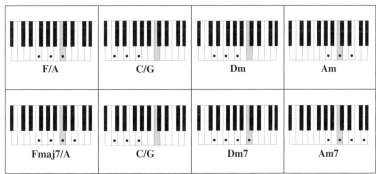

Words and Music by SARAH McLACHLAN,
SEAMUS EGAN and DAVE MERENDA

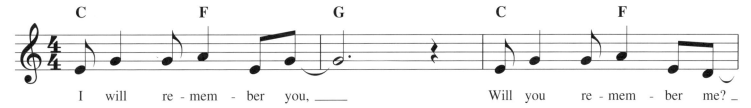

I will re - mem - ber you, _____ Will you re - mem - ber me? _

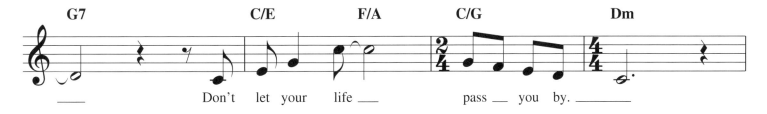

_____ Don't let your life _ pass _ you by. _____

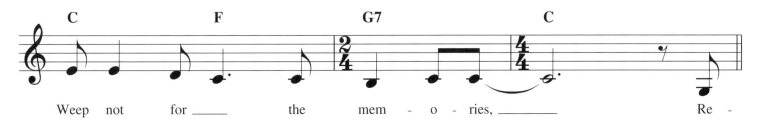

Weep not for _____ the mem - o - ries, _____ Re -

mem - ber the good times that we had. _____ We
I'm so tired, but I can't sleep. ___
so a - fraid to love you, more a - fraid to lose,

66

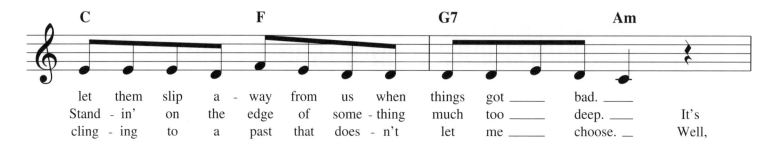

let them slip a - way from us when things got ___ bad. ___
Stand - in' on the edge of some - thing much too ___ deep. ___ It's
cling - ing to a past that does - n't let me ___ choose. ___ Well,

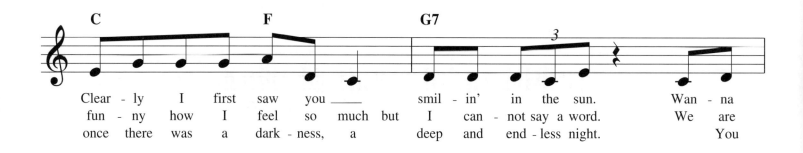

Clear - ly I first saw you ___ smil - in' in the sun. Wan - na
fun - ny how I feel so much but I can - not say a word. We are
once there was a dark - ness, a deep and end - less night. You

feel your warmth up - on me. I wan - na be the one. ___
scream - ing in - side or we can't be heard.
gave me ev - 'ry - thing you had oh, you gave me light. ___

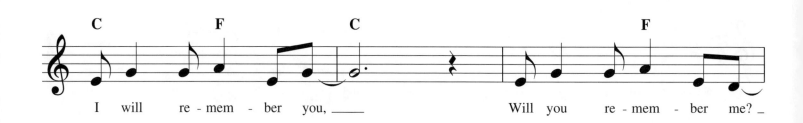

I will re - mem - ber you, ___ Will you re - mem - ber me? _

___ Don't let your life ___ pass ___ you by. ___

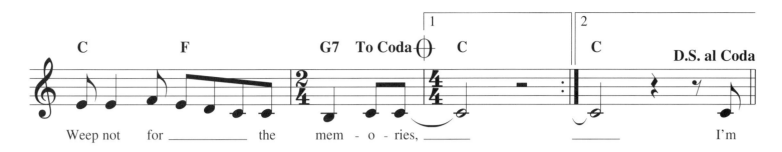

Weep not for _____ the mem - o - ries, _____ _____ I'm

CODA

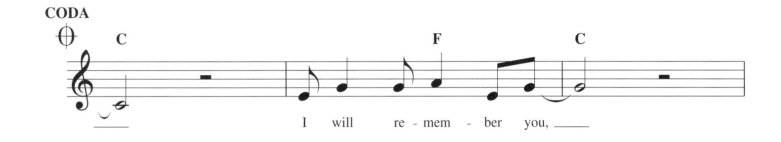

_____ I will re - mem - ber you, _____

Will you re - mem - ber me? _____ Don't let your life _____

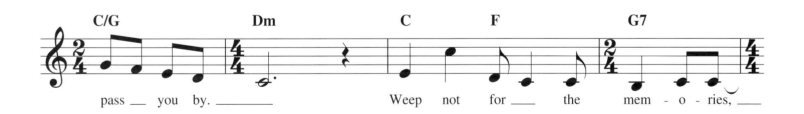

pass __ you by. _____ Weep not for ___ the mem - o - ries, ___

_____ Weep not for _____ the mem - o - ries.

I'VE GOT YOU UNDER MY SKIN
from BORN TO DANCE

Words and Music by
COLE PORTER

I've got you _____ un-der my skin. _____ I've

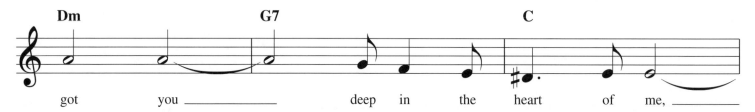

got you _____ deep in the heart of me, _____

_____ so deep in my heart, _____ you're real-ly a

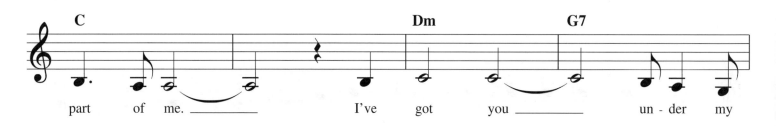

part of me. _____ I've got you _____ un-der my

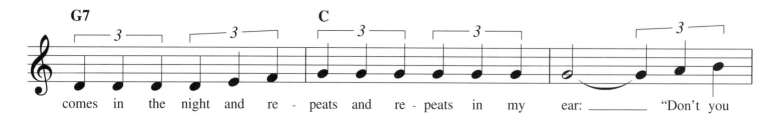

comes in the night and re - peats and re - peats in my ear: _____ "Don't you

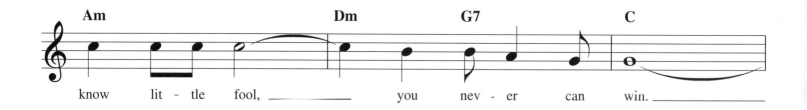

know lit - tle fool, _____ you nev - er can win. _____

___ Use your men - tal - i - ty, _____ wake up to re -

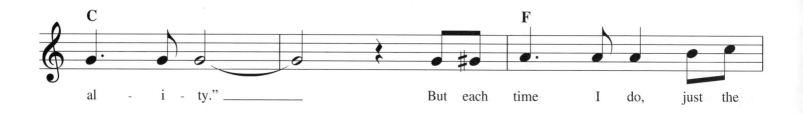

al - i - ty." _____ But each time I do, just the

thought of you makes me stop be - fore I be - gin. 'Cause I've

got you _____ un - der my skin. _____

JINGLE BELLS

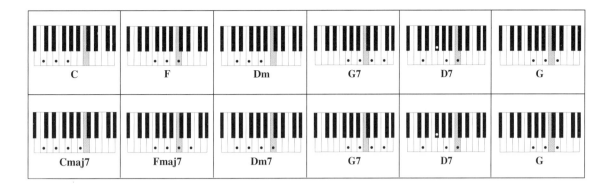

Words and Music by
J. PIERPONT

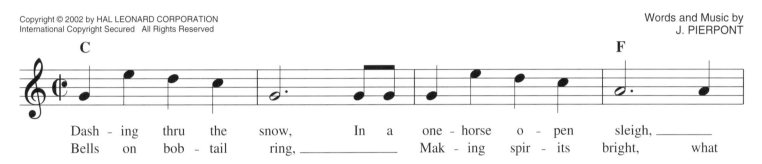

Dash - ing thru the snow, In a one - horse o - pen sleigh, _____
Bells on bob - tail ring, _____ Mak - ing spir - its bright, what

O'er the fields we go, Laugh - ing all the way.
fun it is to

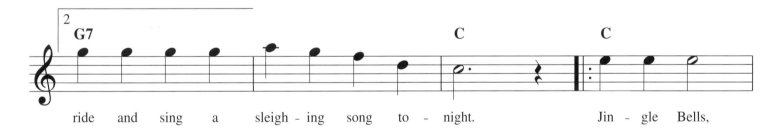

ride and sing a sleigh - ing song to - night. Jin - gle Bells,

Jin - gle Bells, Jin - gle all the way! Oh, what fun it

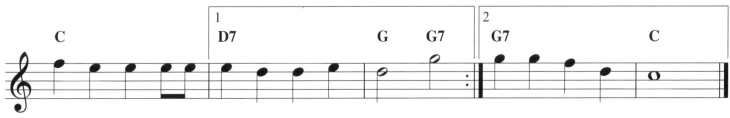

is to ride in a one - horse o - pen sleigh! Oh, one - horse o - pen sleigh.

IF

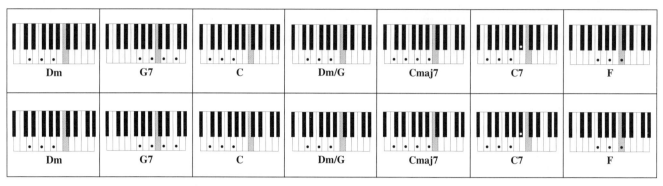

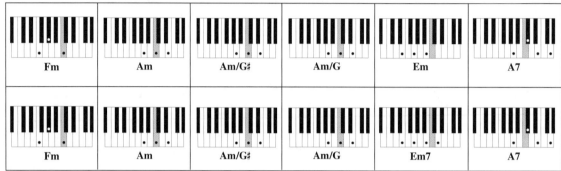

Words and Music by
DAVID GATES

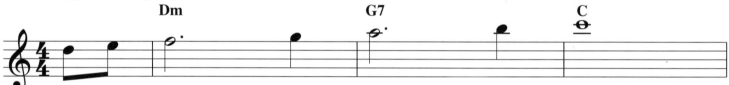

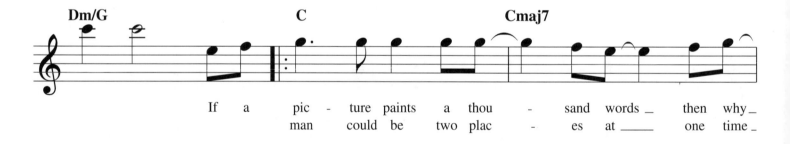

If a pic - ture paints a thou - sand words _ then why _
man could be two plac - es at _____ one time _

_____ can't I _____ paint you? The words _ will nev - er show _
_____ I'd be _ with you; to - mor - row and to - day, _

_____ the you _ I've come _ to know. _ If a
_____ be - side _ you all _ the way. _ If the

IMAGINE

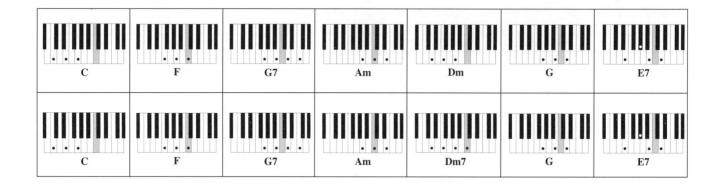

Words and Music by
JOHN LENNON

I - mag - ine there's   no heav - en.

It's eas - y if you   try. _____   No hell ___ be - low

us,   a - bove us on - ly sky.

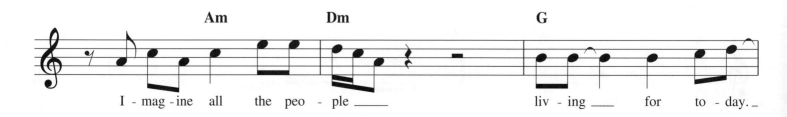

I - mag - ine all   the peo - ple _____   liv - ing ___ for to - day. _

IN A SENTIMENTAL MOOD

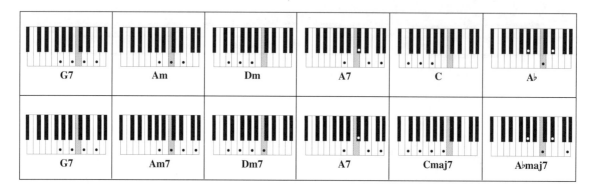

Words and Music by DUKE ELLINGTON,
IRVING MILLS and MANNY KURTZ

In a sen - ti - men - tal

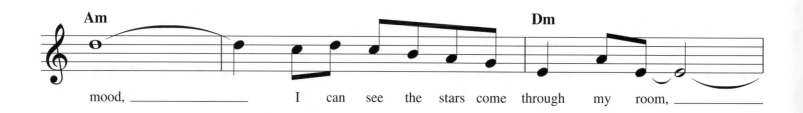

mood, _____ I can see the stars come through my room, _____

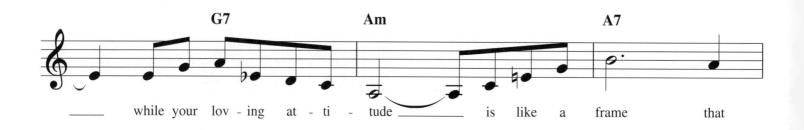

_____ while your lov - ing at - ti - tude _____ is like a frame that

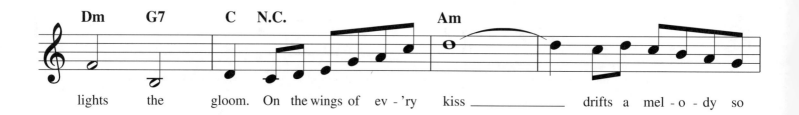

lights the gloom. On the wings of ev - 'ry kiss _____ drifts a mel - o - dy so

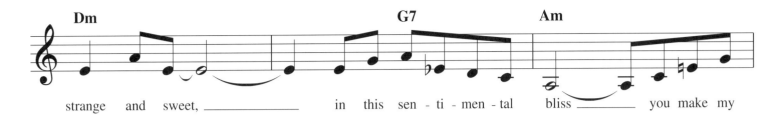

strange and sweet, _____ in this sen - ti - men - tal bliss _____ you make my

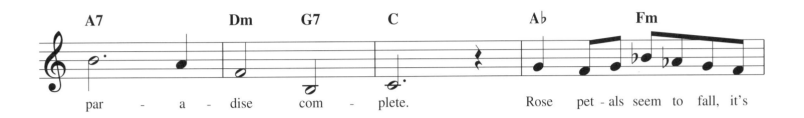

par - a - dise com - plete. Rose pet - als seem to fall, it's

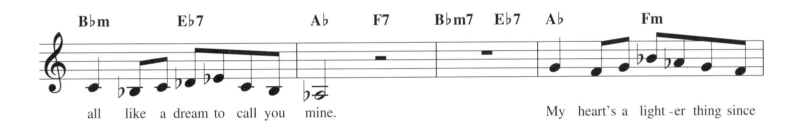

all like a dream to call you mine. My heart's a light - er thing since

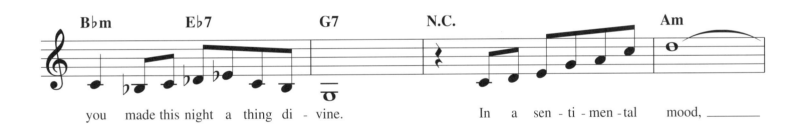

you made this night a thing di - vine. In a sen - ti - men - tal mood, _____

_____ I'm with - in a world so heav - en - ly, _____ for I nev - er dreamt that

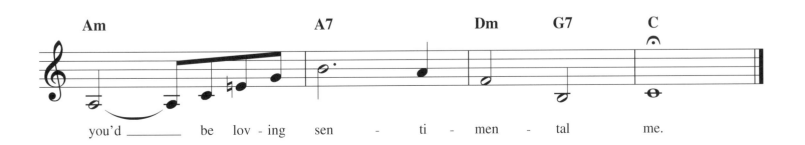

you'd _____ be lov - ing sen - ti - men - tal me.

ISN'T IT ROMANTIC?
from the Paramount Picture LOVE ME TONIGHT

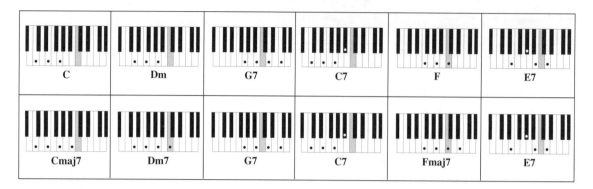

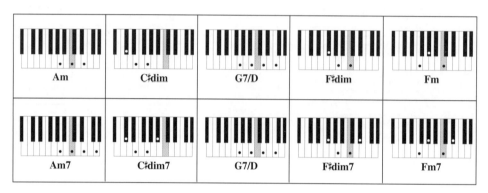

Words by LORENZ HART
Music by RICHARD RODGERS

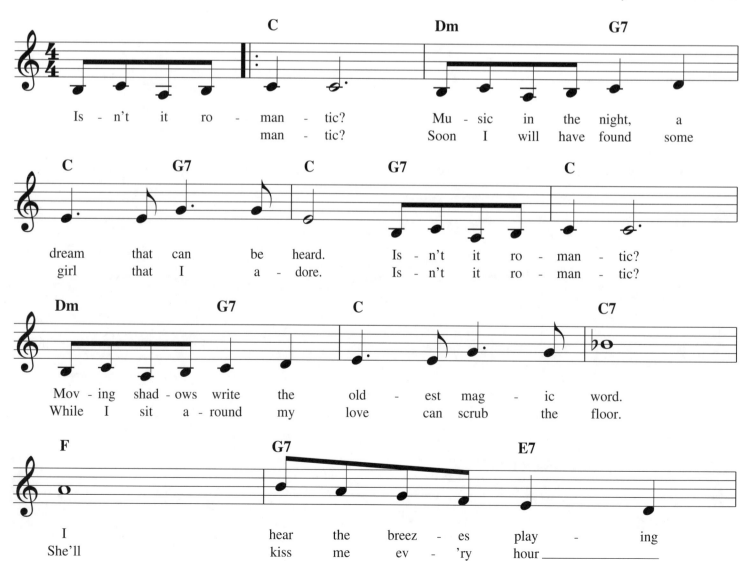

Is - n't it ro - man - tic? Mu - sic in the night, a
man - tic? Soon I will have found some

dream that can be heard. Is - n't it ro - man - tic?
girl that I a - dore. Is - n't it ro - man - tic?

Mov - ing shad - ows write the old - est mag - ic word.
While I sit a - round my love can scrub the floor.

I hear the breez - es play - ing
She'll kiss me ev - 'ry hour _____

IT CAME UPON THE MIDNIGHT CLEAR

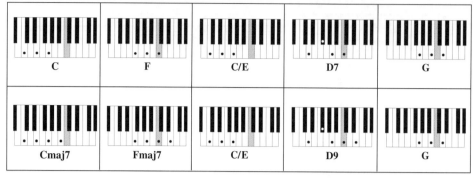

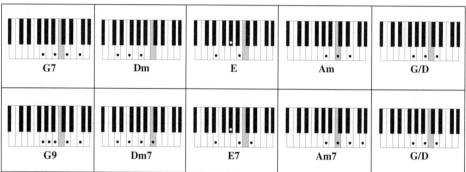

Words by EDMUND HAMILTON SEARS
Music by RICHARD STORRS WILLIS

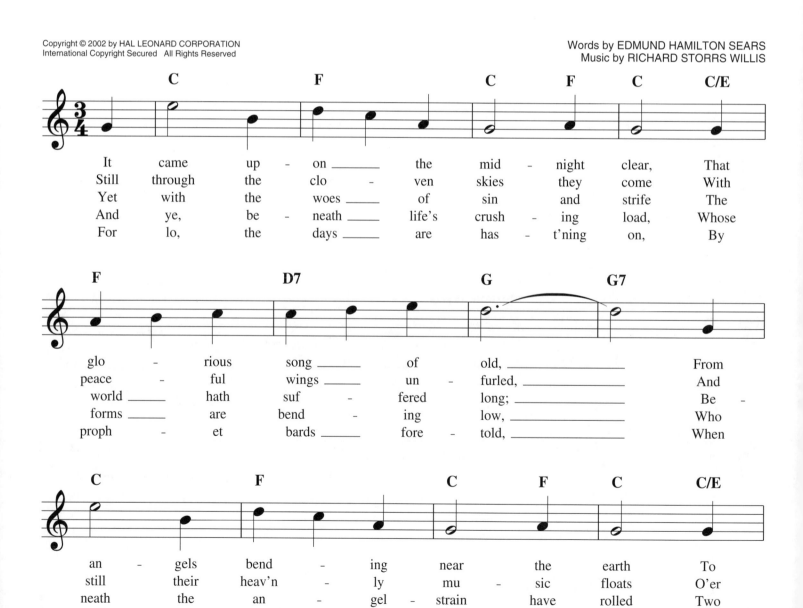

It	came	up - on	the	mid -	night	clear,	That
Still	through	the clo -	ven	skies	they	come	With
Yet	with	the woes	of	sin	and	strife	The
And	ye,	be - neath	life's	crush -	ing	load,	Whose
For	lo,	the days	are	has -	t'ning	on,	By

glo -	rious	song	of	old,	From
peace -	ful	wings	un -	furled,	And
world	hath	suf -	fered	long;	Be -
forms	are	bend -	ing	low,	Who
proph -	et	bards	fore -	told,	When

an -	gels	bend -	ing	near	the	earth	To
still	their	heav'n -	ly	mu -	sic	floats	O'er
neath	the	an -	gel -	strain	have	rolled	Two
toil	a -	long	the	climb -	ing	way	With
with	the	ev -	er -	cir -	cling	years	Comes

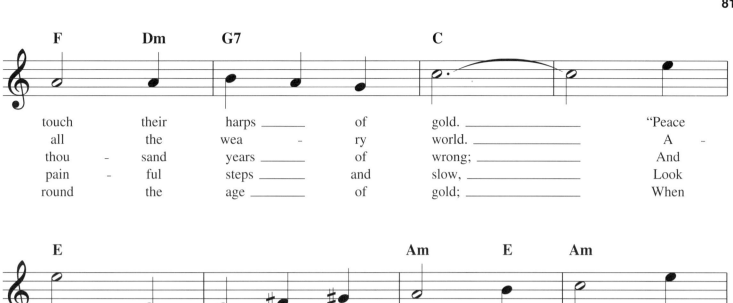

touch their harps _____ of gold. _____ "Peace
all the wea - ry world. _____ A -
thou - sand years _____ of wrong; _____ And
pain - ful steps _____ and slow, _____ Look
round the age _____ of gold; _____ When

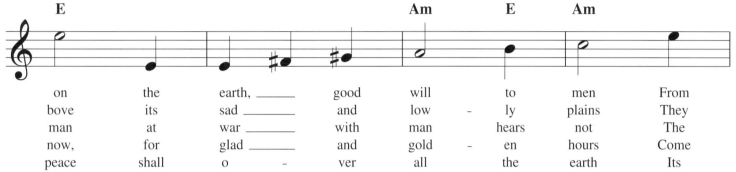

on the earth, _____ good will to men From
bove its sad _____ and low - ly plains They
man at war _____ with man hears not The
now, for glad _____ and gold - en hours Come
peace shall o - ver all the earth Its

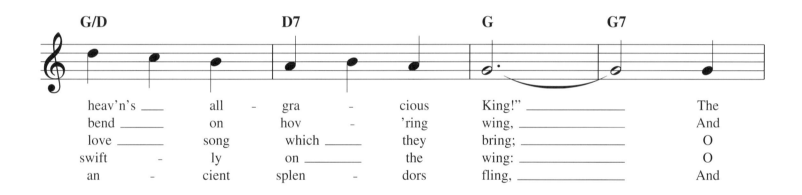

heav'n's _____ all - gra - cious King!" _____ The
bend _____ on hov - 'ring wing, _____ And
love _____ song which _____ they bring; _____ O
swift - ly on _____ the wing: _____ O
an - cient splen - dors fling, _____ And

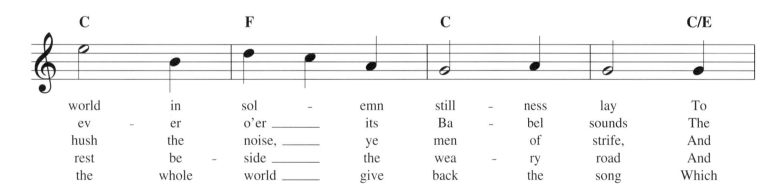

world in sol - emn still - ness lay To
ev - er o'er _____ its Ba - bel sounds The
hush the noise, _____ ye men of strife, And
rest be - side _____ the wea - ry road And
the whole world _____ give back the song Which

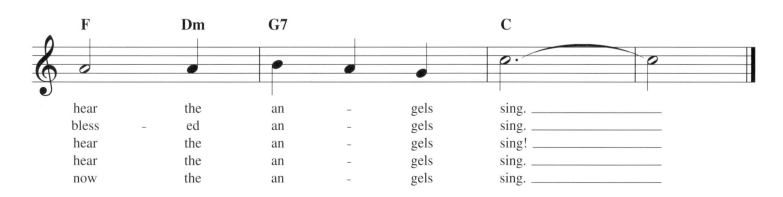

hear the an - gels sing. _____
bless - ed an - gels sing. _____
hear the an - gels sing! _____
hear the an - gels sing. _____
now the an - gels sing. _____

IT'S ONLY A PAPER MOON

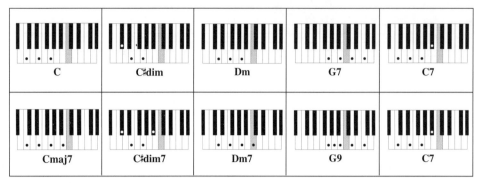

Lyric by BILLY ROSE and E.Y. HARBURG
Music by HAROLD ARLEN

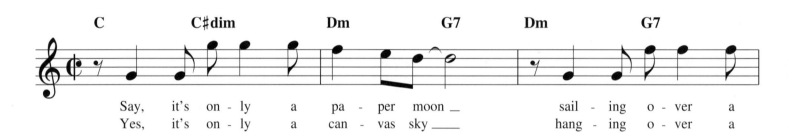

Say, it's on-ly a pa-per moon _ sail-ing o-ver a
Yes, it's on-ly a can-vas sky ____ hang-ing o-ver a

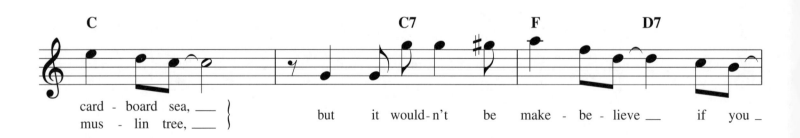

card-board sea, ___ } but it would-n't be make-be-lieve ___ if you ___
mus-lin tree, ___ }

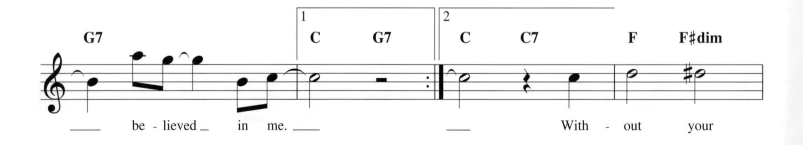

___ be-lieved _ in me. ___ With-out your

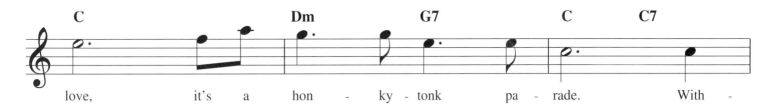

love, it's a hon - ky - tonk pa - rade. With -

out your love, it's a mel - o - dy played in a

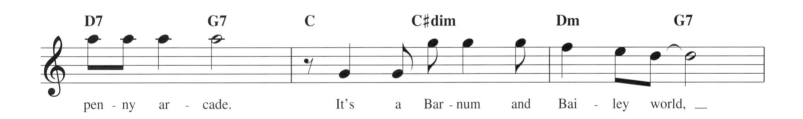

pen - ny ar - cade. It's a Bar - num and Bai - ley world, __

just as pho - ny as it can be, ____ but it would -n't be

make - be - lieve __ if you ____ be - lieved __ in me. ____

JAILHOUSE ROCK

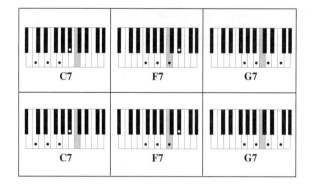

Words and Music by JERRY LEIBER
and MIKE STOLLER

1. The war-den threw a par-ty in the
2. - 5. *(See additional lyrics)*

coun-ty jail. The pris-on band was there and they be-gan to wail. The

band was jump-in' and the joint be-gan to swing. You should have heard those knocked-out

Chorus

jail-birds sing. Let's rock! Ev-'ry-bod-y let's

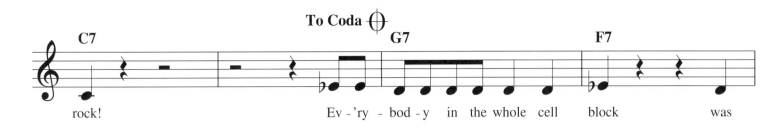

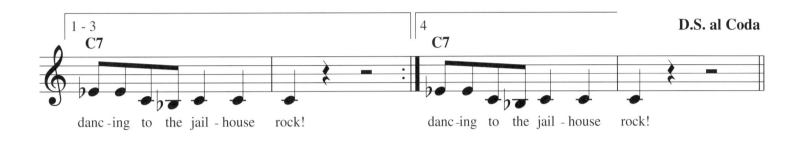

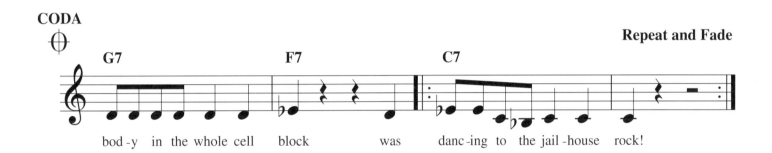

Additional Lyrics

2. Spider Murphy played the tenor saxophone
   Little Joe was blowin' on the slide trombone,
   The drummer boy from Illinois went crash, boom, bang;
   The whole rhythm section was the Purple Gang.
   (Chorus)

3. Number Forty-seven said to number Three;
   "You're the cutest jailbird I ever did see.
   I sure would be delighted with your company,
   Come on and do the Jailhouse Rock with me."
   (Chorus)

4. The sad sack was a-sittin' on a block of stone,
   Way over in the corner weeping all alone.
   The warden said: "Hey Buddy, don't you be so square,
   If you can't find a partner, use a wooden chair!"
   (Chorus)

5. Shifty Henry said to Bugs: "For heaven's sake,
   No one's lookin', now's our chance to make a break."
   Bugsy turned to Shifty and he said: "Nix, nix;
   I wanna stick around awhile and get my kicks."
   (Chorus)

JINGLE-BELL ROCK

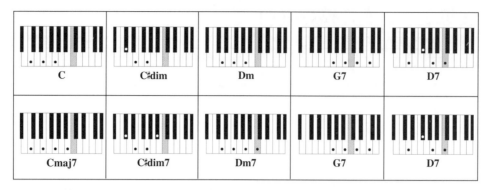

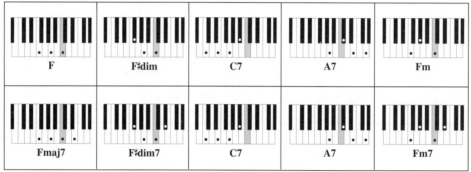

Words and Music by JOE BEAL
and JIM BOOTHE

Jin - gle - bell, jin - gle - bell, jin - gle - bell rock jin - gle - bell swing and

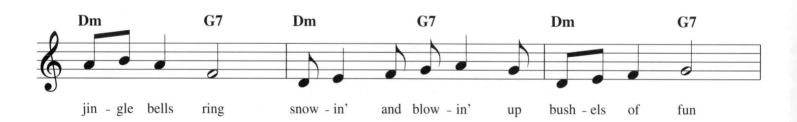

jin - gle bells ring snow - in' and blow - in' up bush - els of fun

Now the jin - gle - hop has be - gun. Jin - gle - bell, jin - gle - bell,

jin - gle - bell rock jin - gle bells chime in jin - gle - bell time,

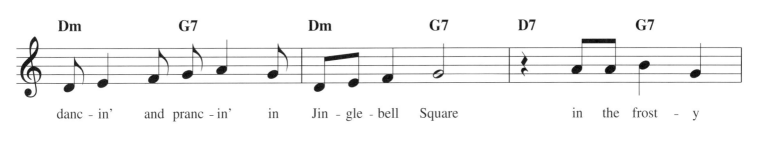

danc - in'   and pranc - in'   in   Jin - gle - bell   Square   in   the   frost - y

air.   What   a   bright ___   time ___   it's   the   right ___   time ___   to

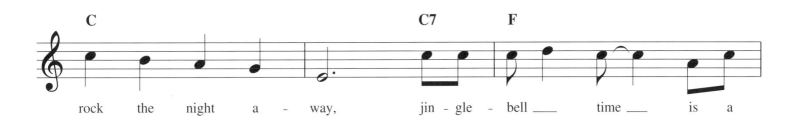

rock   the   night   a - way,   jin - gle - bell ___   time ___   is   a

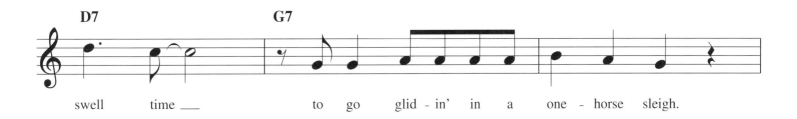

swell   time ___   to   go   glid - in'   in   a   one - horse   sleigh.

Gid - dy - up,   jin - gle - horse   pick   up   your   feet   jin - gle   a - round   the

clock;   Mix   and   min - gle   in   a   jin - gl - in'   beat   that's   the   jin - gle - bell

rock.   that's   the   jin - gle - bell,   that's   the   jin - gle - bell   rock.

JOY TO THE WORLD

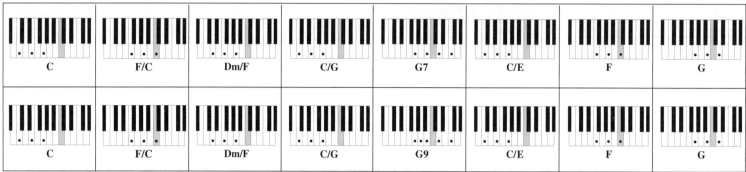

Words by ISAAC WATTS
Music by GEORGE FRIDERIC HANDEL
Arranged by LOWELL MASON

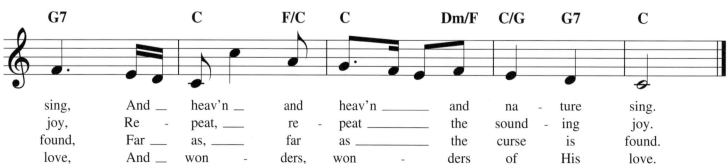

LET IT BE

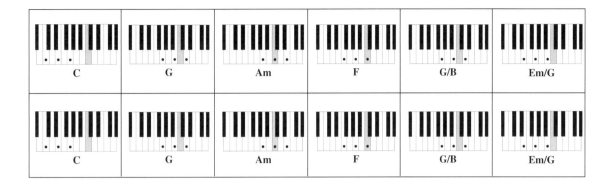

Words and Music by JOHN LENNON
and PAUL McCARTNEY

When I find my-self in times of trou-ble Moth-er Ma-ry comes to me,
when the bro-ken-heart-ed peo-ple liv-ing in the world a-gree,

speak-ing words of wis-dom, let it be. _____ And
there will be an an-swer, let it be. _____ For

in my hour of dark-ness she is stand-ing right in front of me. Speak-ing words of wis-dom, let it
though they may be part-ed, there is still a chance that they will see. There will be an an-swer, let it

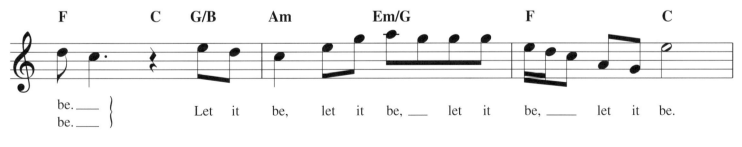

be. _____ Let it be, let it be, ____ let it be, ____ let it be.
be. _____

Whis-per words of wis-dom, let it be. _____ And
There will be an an-swer, let it be. _____

KANSAS CITY

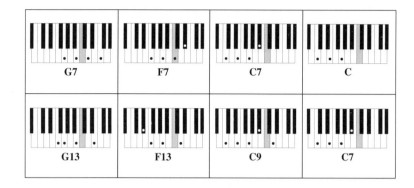

Words and Music by JERRY LEIBER
and MIKE STOLLER

I'm go-in' to

Kan-sas Cit-y, Kan-sas Cit-y here I come. _____ I'm go-in' to

Kan-sas Cit-y, Kan-sas Cit-y here I come. _____ They got a

cra-zy way of lov-in' there and I'm gon-na get me some. _____

_____ I'm gon-na be stand-in' on the cor-ner Twelfth Street and Vine. _
pack my clothes, _ leave at the crack of dawn. _

MANDY

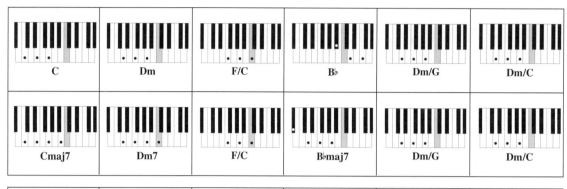

Words and Music by SCOTT ENGLISH
and RICHARD KERR

I re- mem- ber all my life _____
morn- ing's just an- oth- er day; _____
stand- ing on the edge of time; _____ I've

rain- ing down as cold as ice. _____
hap- py peo- ple pass my way. _____
walked a- way when love was mine.

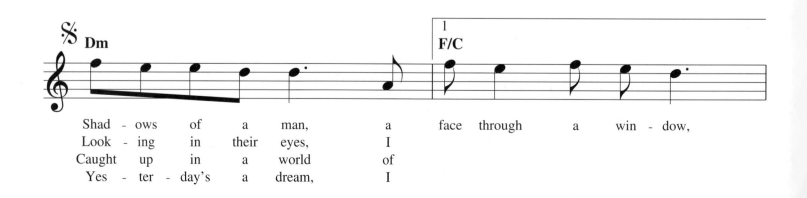

Shad- ows of a man, a face through a win- dow,
Look- ing in their eyes, I
Caught up in a world of
Yes- ter- day's a dream, I

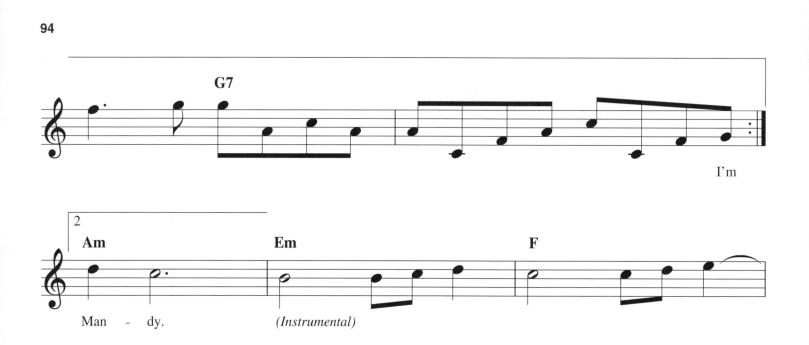

G7

I'm

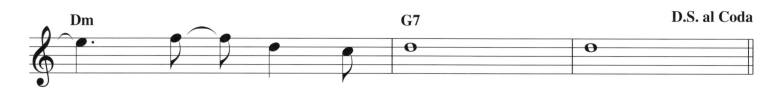

2

Am   Em   F

Man - dy.   (Instrumental)

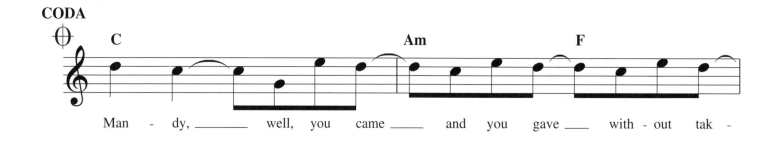

Dm   G7   D.S. al Coda

CODA

C   Am   F

Man - dy, _____ well, you came ____ and you gave ____ with - out tak -

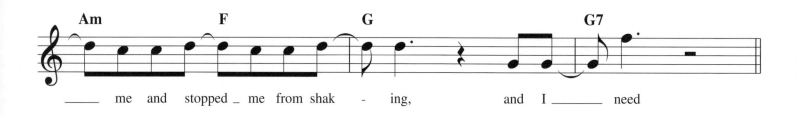

G   G7   C

- ing, but I sent ____ you a - way. _ Oh Man - dy, well, you kissed _

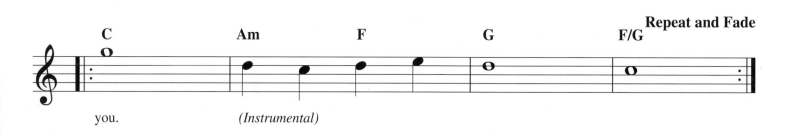

Am   F   G   G7

____ me and stopped _ me from shak - ing, and I _____ need

Repeat and Fade

C   Am   F   G   F/G

you.   (Instrumental)

LET IT SNOW! LET IT SNOW! LET IT SNOW!

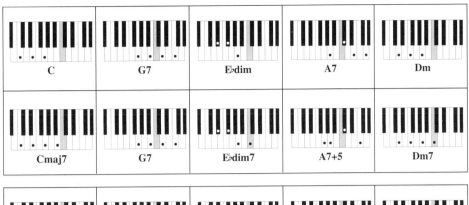

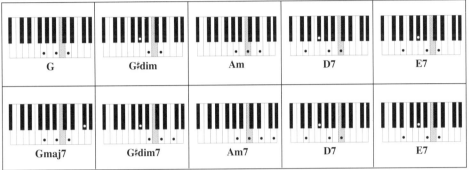

Words by SAMMY CAHN
Music by JULE STYNE

MICHELLE

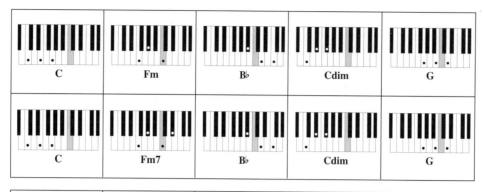

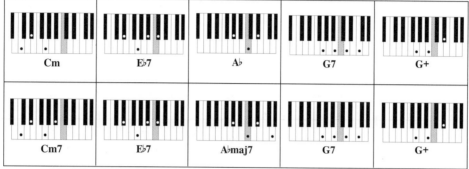

Words and Music by JOHN LENNON
and PAUL McCARTNEY

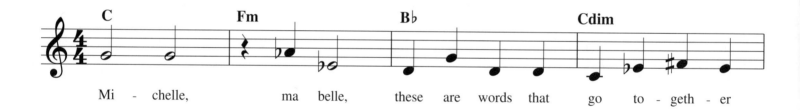

Mi - chelle, ma belle, these are words that go to - geth - er

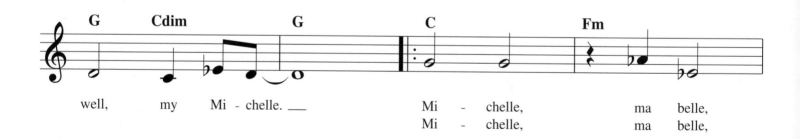

well, my Mi - chelle. ___

Mi - chelle, ma belle,
Mi - chelle, ma belle,

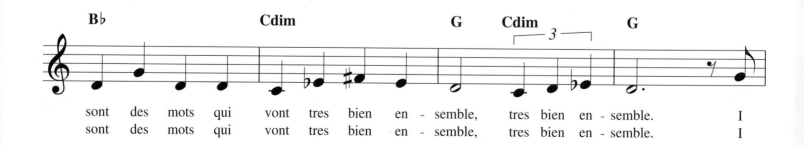

sont des mots qui vont tres bien en - semble, tres bien en - semble.   I
sont des mots qui vont tres bien en - semble, tres bien en - semble.   I

love you, I love you, I love you, that's all I want to
need to, I need to, I need to, I need to make you

say. Un - til I find a way _____ I will
see. Oh, what ___ you mean to me _____ un -

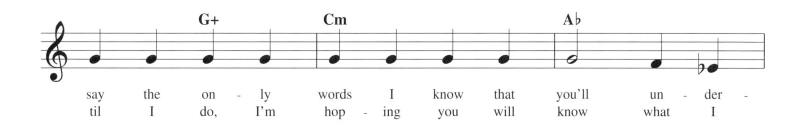

say the on - ly words I know that you'll un - der -
til I do, I'm hop - ing you will know what I

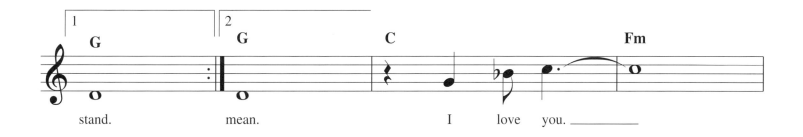

stand. mean. I love you. _____

(Instrumental)

I want you, I want you, I want _____ you,

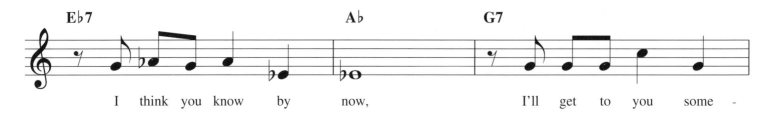

I think you know by now, I'll get to you some -

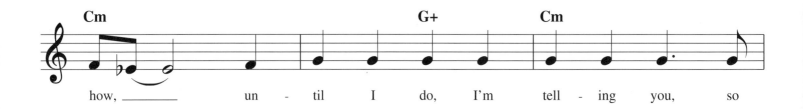

how, _____ un - til I do, I'm tell - ing you, so

you'll un - der - stand; Mi - chelle, ma belle,

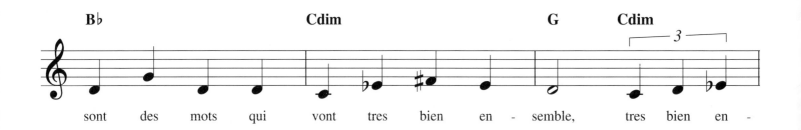

sont des mots qui vont tres bien en - semble, tres bien en -

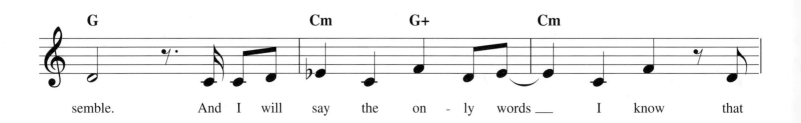

semble. And I will say the on - ly words ___ I know that

you'll un - der - stand, my Mi - chelle. _____

O CHRISTMAS TREE

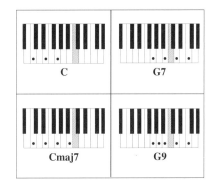

Traditional German Carol

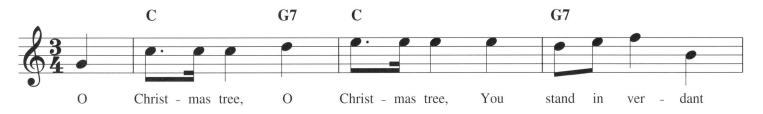

O   Christ - mas tree,   O   Christ - mas tree,   You   stand   in   ver - dant

beau - ty!   O   Christ - mas tree,   O   Christ - mas tree,   You

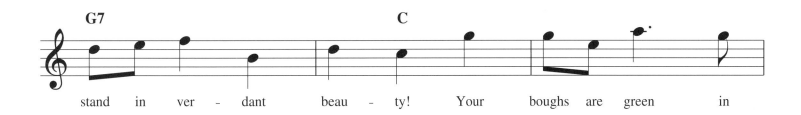

stand   in   ver - dant   beau - ty!   Your   boughs   are   green   in

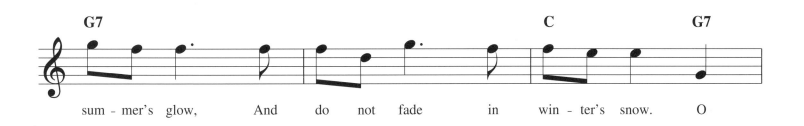

sum - mer's glow,   And   do   not   fade   in   win - ter's   snow.   O

Christ - mas tree,   O   Christ - mas tree,   You   stand   in   ver - dant   beau - ty!

MISTY

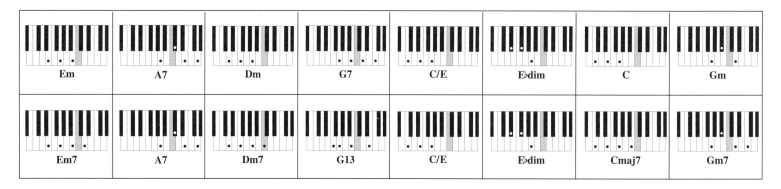

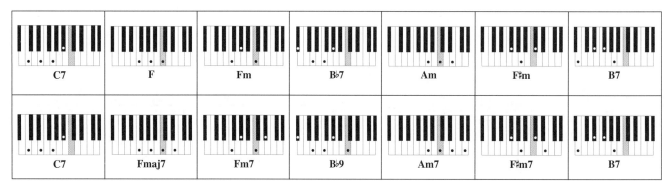

Words by JOHNNY BURKE
Music by ERROLL GARNER

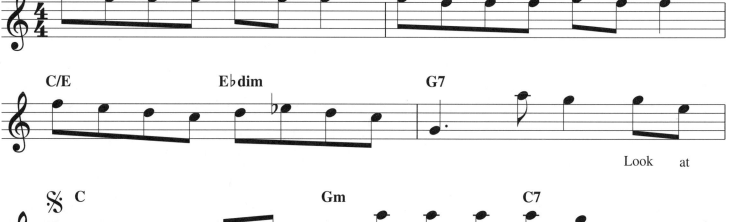

Look at

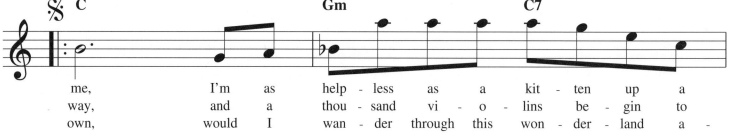

me,   I'm as   help - less   as a   kit - ten   up   a
way,   and a   thou - sand   vi - o - lins   be - gin   to
own,   would I   wan - der   through this   won - der - land   a -

tree,   and I   feel   like   I'm   cling - ing   to   a   cloud,   I
play,   or it   might   be   the   sound   of   your   hel - lo,   that
lone,   nev - er   know - ing   my   right   foot   from   my   left,   my

To Coda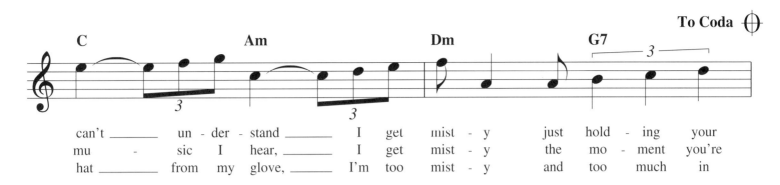

can't _____ un - der - stand _____ I get mist - y just hold - ing your
mu - sic I hear, _____ I get mist - y the mo - ment you're
hat _____ from my glove, _____ I'm too mist - y and too much in

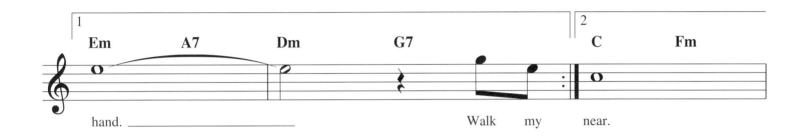

hand. _____ Walk my near.

You can say that you're lead - ing me on, ____

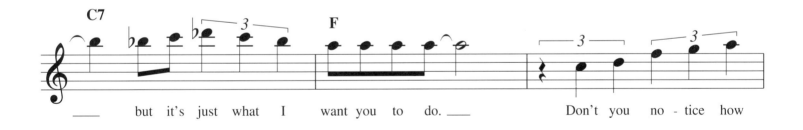

____ but it's just what I want you to do. ___ Don't you no - tice how

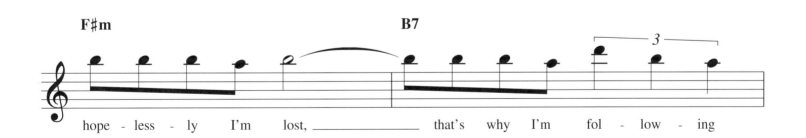

hope - less - ly I'm lost, _____ that's why I'm fol - low - ing

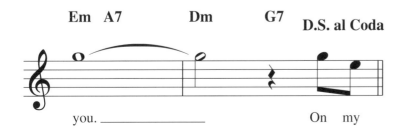

you. ____ On my

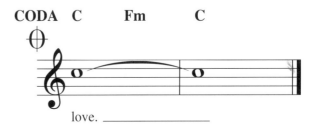

love. ____

MOOD INDIGO
from SOPHISTICATED LADIES

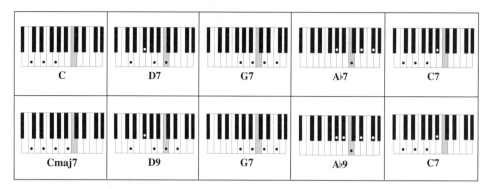

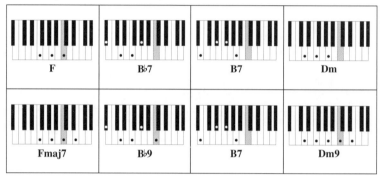

Words and Music by DUKE ELLINGTON,
IRVING MILLS and ALBANY BIGARD

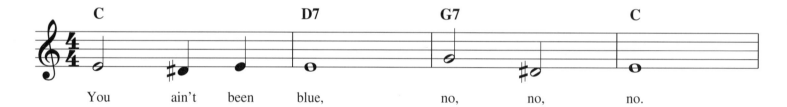

You ain't been blue, no, no, no.

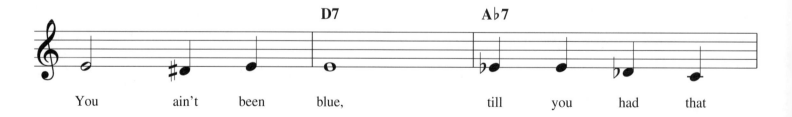

You ain't been blue, till you had that

mood in - di - go. That feel - in' goes steal - in'

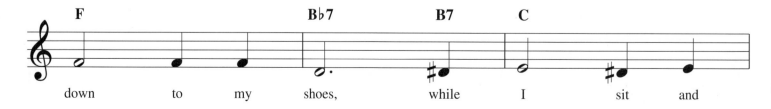

down to my shoes, while I sit and

MOON RIVER
from the Paramount Picture BREAKFAST AT TIFFANY'S

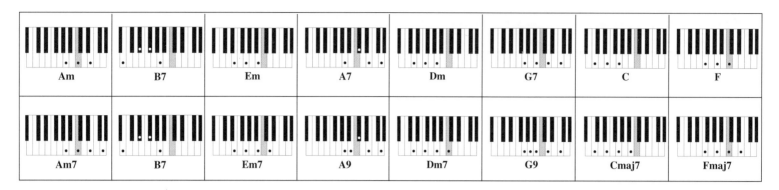

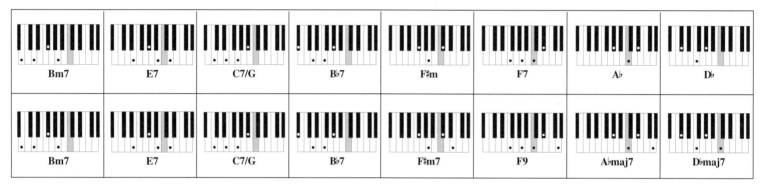

Words by JOHNNY MERCER
Music by HENRY MANCINI

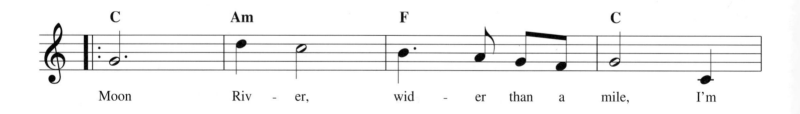

Moon Riv - er, wid - er than a mile, I'm

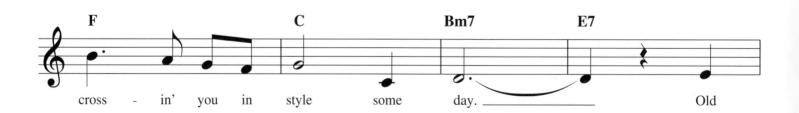

cross - in' you in style some day. _____ Old

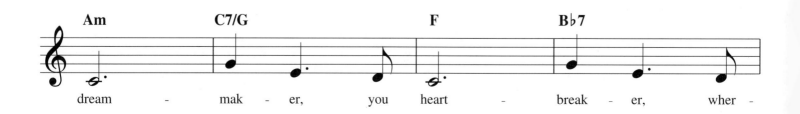

dream - mak - er, you heart - break - er, wher -

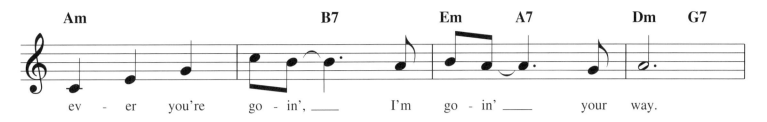

Am .... **B7** ..... **Em** ..... **A7** ..... **Dm** **G7**

ev - er you're go - in', ____ I'm go - in' ____ your way.

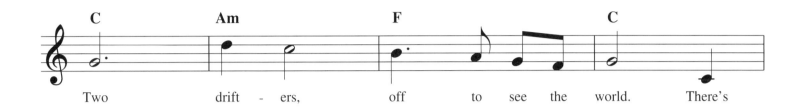

C ..... **Am** ..... **F** ..... **C**

Two drift - ers, off to see the world. There's

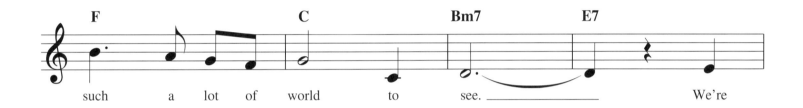

F ..... **C** ..... **Bm7** **E7**

such a lot of world to see. ____ We're

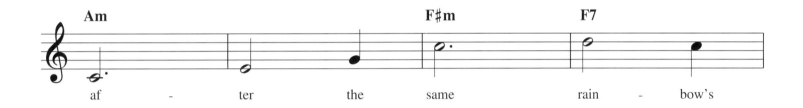

Am ..... **F♯m** **F7**

af - ter the same rain - bow's

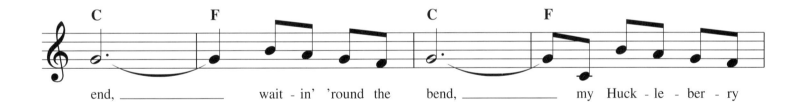

C ..... **F** ..... **C** ..... **F**

end, ____ wait - in' 'round the bend, ____ my Huck - le - ber - ry

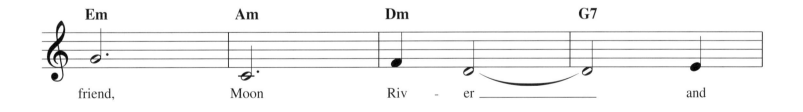

Em ..... **Am** ..... **Dm** **G7**

friend, Moon Riv - er ____ and

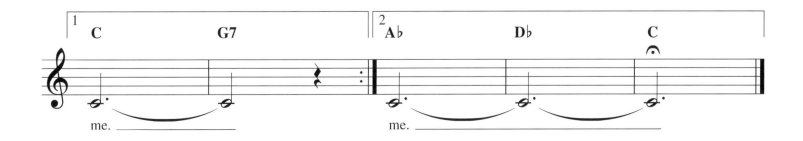

1 **C** ..... **G7** ..... **2** **A♭** ..... **D♭** ..... **C**

me. ____ me. ____

MOONGLOW

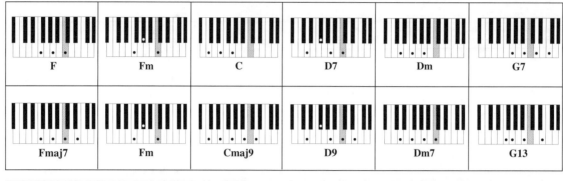

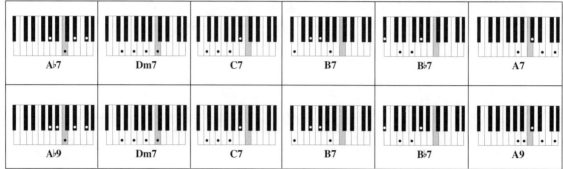

Words and Music by WILL HUDSON,
EDDIE DE LANGE and IRVING MILLS

It must have been moon - glow,   way up in the

blue,   it must have been moon - glow

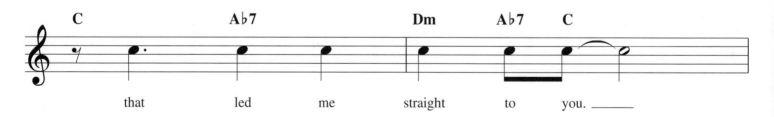

that   led   me   straight   to   you. _____

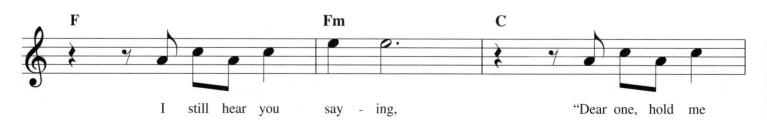

I still hear you say - ing,   "Dear one, hold me

107

fast." And I start in pray - ing,

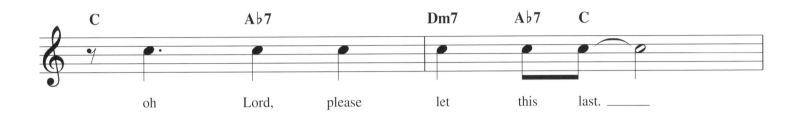

oh Lord, please let this last. _____

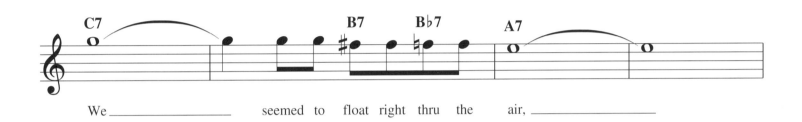

We _____ seemed to float right thru the air, _____

heav - en - ly songs _____ seemed to come from ev - 'ry - where:

And now when there's moon - glow way up in the

blue, I al - ways re - mem - ber

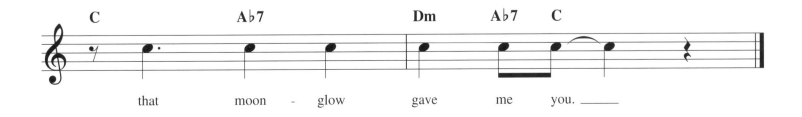

that moon - glow gave me you. _____

MOONLIGHT IN VERMONT

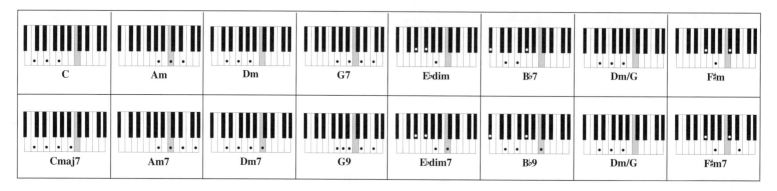

Words and Music by JOHN BLACKBURN
and KARL SUESSDORF

Pen - nies in a stream,

fall - ing leaves a sy - ca - more, moon - light in Ver -

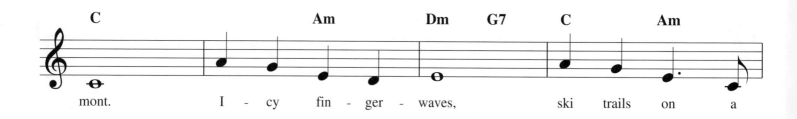

mont. I - cy fin - ger waves, ski trails on a

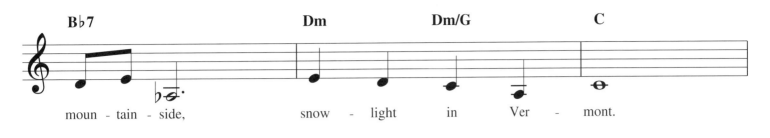

moun - tain - side, snow - light in Ver - mont.

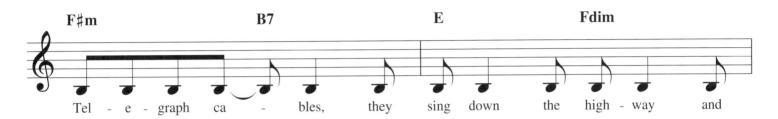

Tel - e - graph ca - bles, they sing down the high - way and

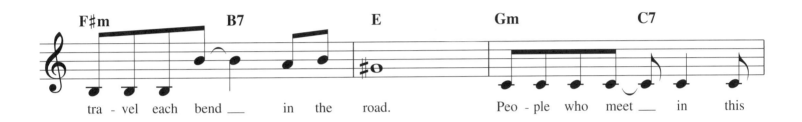

tra - vel each bend __ in the road. Peo - ple who meet __ in this

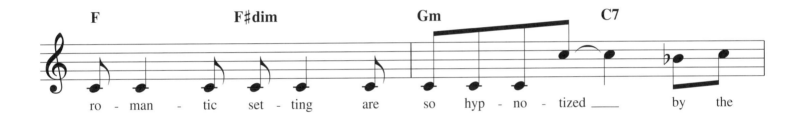

ro - man - tic set - ting are so hyp - no - tized __ by the

love - ly ev' - ning sum - mer breeze,

warb - ling of a mea - dow - lark, moon - light in Ver -

mont, you and I and moon - light in Ver - mont.

MY FAVORITE THINGS
from THE SOUND OF MUSIC

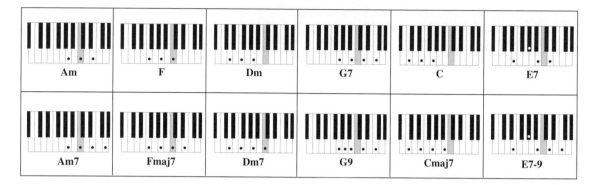

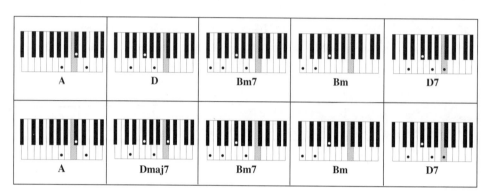

Lyrics by OSCAR HAMMERSTEIN II
Music by RICHARD RODGERS

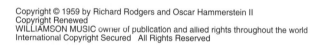

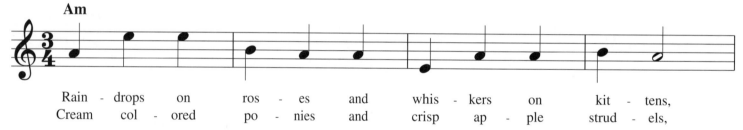

Rain - drops on ros - es and whis - kers on kit - tens,
Cream col - ored po - nies and crisp ap - ple strud - els,

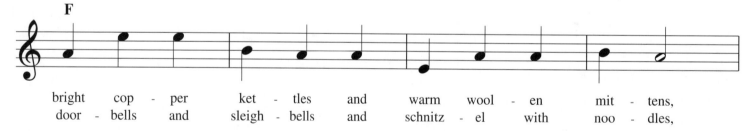

bright cop - per ket - tles and warm wool - en mit - tens,
door - bells and sleigh - bells and schnitz - el with noo - dles,

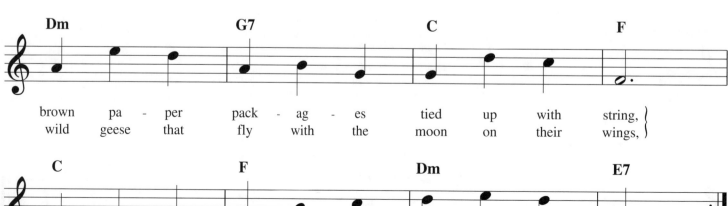

brown pa - per pack - ag - es tied up with string,
wild geese that fly with the moon on their wings,

these are a few of my fa - vor - ite things.

111

MY FUNNY VALENTINE
from BABES IN ARMS

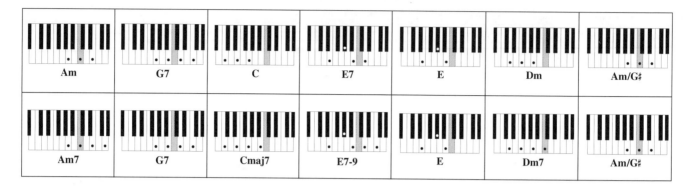

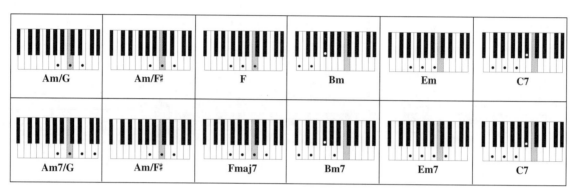

Words by LORENZ HART
Music by RICHARD RODGERS

Be - hold the way our fine feath - ered friend his

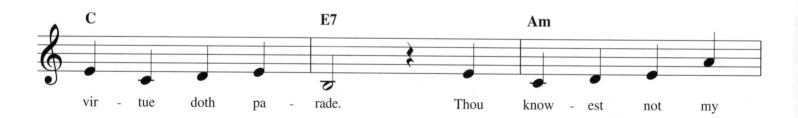

vir - tue doth pa - rade. Thou know - est not my

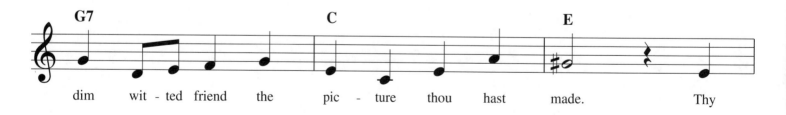

dim wit - ted friend the pic - ture thou hast made. Thy

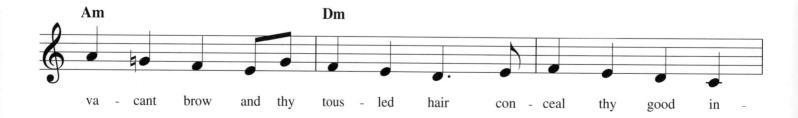

va - cant brow and thy tous - led hair con - ceal thy good in -

tent, thou no - ble, up - right, truth - ful, sin - cere and slight - ly dop - ey

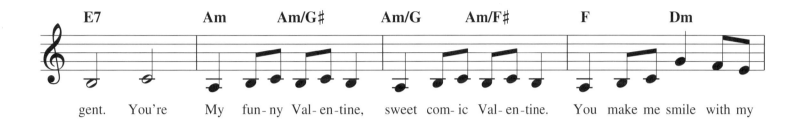

gent. You're My fun - ny Val - en - tine, sweet com - ic Val - en - tine. You make me smile with my

heart. Your looks are laugh - a - ble, un - pho - to - graph - a - ble,

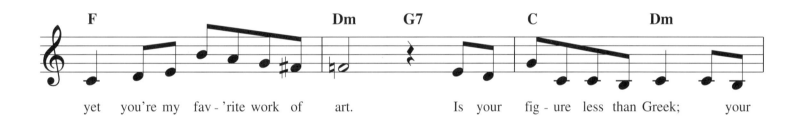

yet you're my fav - 'rite work of art. Is your fig - ure less than Greek; your

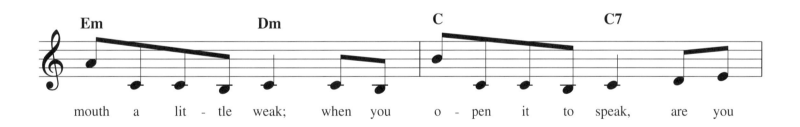

mouth a lit - tle weak; when you o - pen it to speak, are you

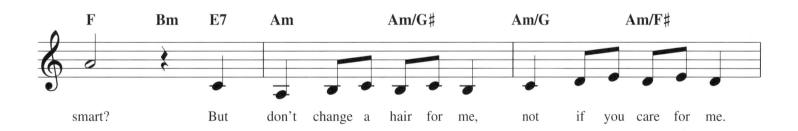

smart? But don't change a hair for me, not if you care for me.

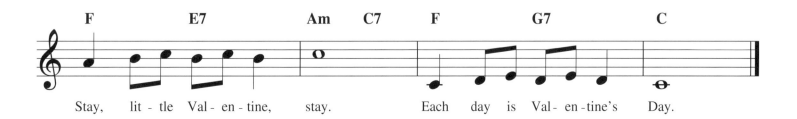

Stay, lit - tle Val - en - tine, stay. Each day is Val - en - tine's Day.

MY ROMANCE
from JUMBO

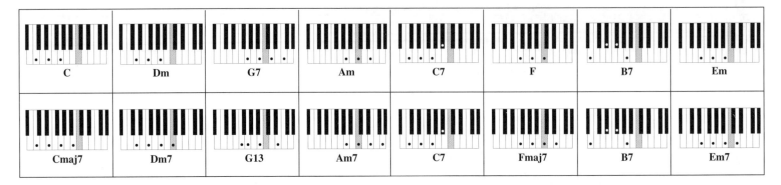

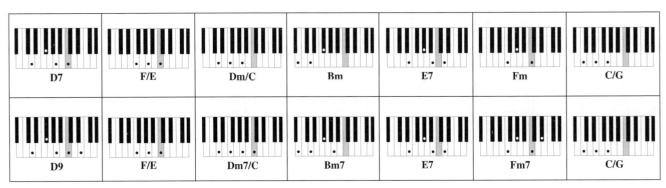

Words by LORENZ HART
Music by RICHARD RODGERS

My ro - mance does -n't have to have a moon in the sky. My ro -

mance does -n't need a blue la - goon stand - ing by; no

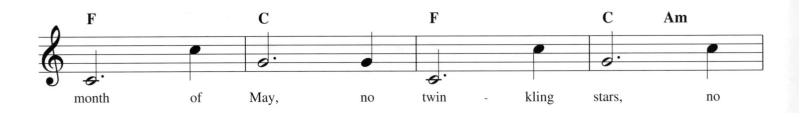

month of May, no twin - kling stars, no

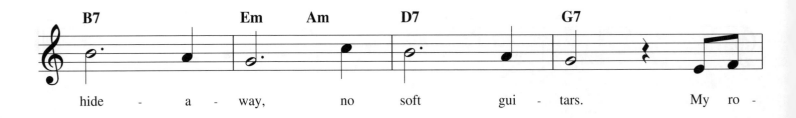

hide - a - way, no soft gui - tars. My ro -

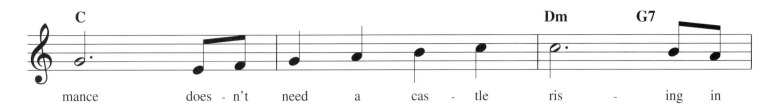

mance does - n't need a cas - tle ris - ing in

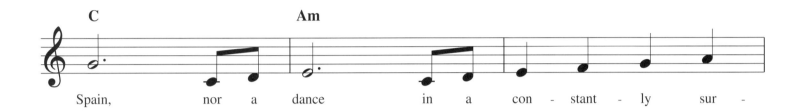

Spain, nor a dance in a con - stant - ly sur -

pris - ing re - frain. Wide a - wake I can

make my most fan - tas - tic dreams come true; my ro -

mance does - n't need a thing but you. _____

A NIGHTINGALE SANG IN BERKELEY SQUARE

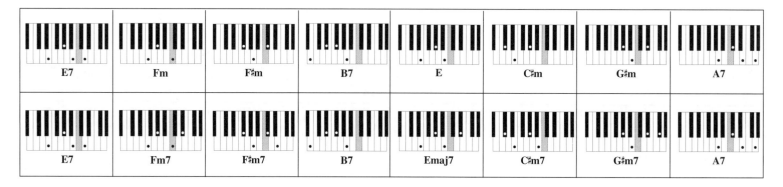

Lyric by ERIC MASCHWITZ
Music by MANNING SHERWIN

O COME, ALL YE FAITHFUL
(Adeste Fideles)

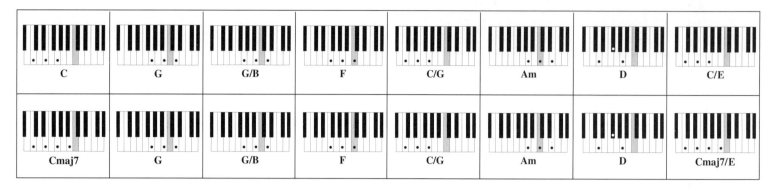

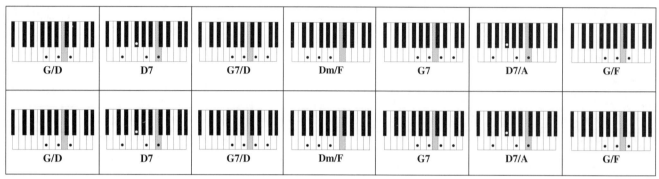

Words and Music by JOHN FRANCIS WADE
Latin Words translated by FREDERICK OAKELEY

O LITTLE TOWN OF BETHLEHEM

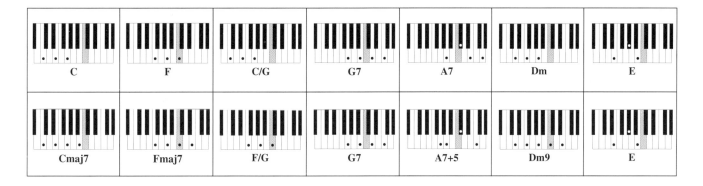

C | F | C/G | G7 | A7 | Dm | E

Cmaj7 | Fmaj7 | F/G | G7 | A7+5 | Dm9 | E

Words by PHILLIPS BROOKS
Music by LEWIS H. REDNER

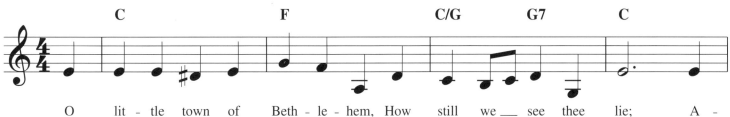

O   lit - tle   town   of   Beth - le - hem, How   still   we __ see   thee   lie;   A -
For   Christ is   born   of   Mar -   y,   And   gath - ered __ all   a - bove,   While
How   si - lent - ly,   how   si - lent - ly   The   won - drous __ gift   is   giv'n!   So
O   ho - ly   Child   of   Beth - le - hem, De - scend   to __ us,   we   pray;   Cast

bove   thy   deep   and   dream - less   sleep   The   si - lent __ stars   go   by.   Yet
mor - tals   sleep, the   an - gels   keep   Their   watch   of __ won - d'ring   love.   O
God   im - parts   to   hu - man   hearts   The   bless - ings __ of   His   heav'n.   No
out   our   sin   and   en - ter   in;   Be   born   in __ us   to - day.   We

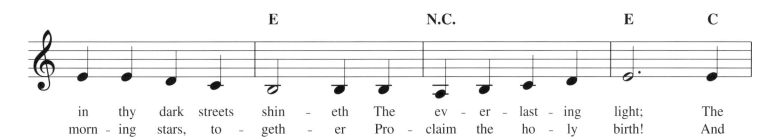

in   thy   dark   streets   shin - eth   The   ev - er - last - ing   light;   The
morn - ing   stars,   to - geth -   er   Pro - claim   the   ho - ly   birth!   And
ear   may   hear   His   com -   ing,   But   in   this   world   of   sin,   Where
hear   the   Christ - mas   an -   gels   The   great   glad   tid - ings   tell;   O

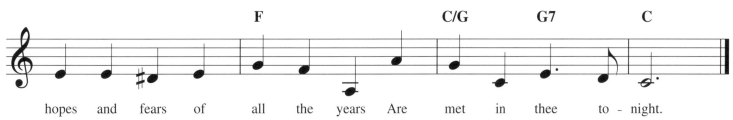

hopes   and   fears   of   all   the   years   Are   met   in   thee   to - night.
prais - es   sing   to   God   the   King,   And   peace   to   men   on   earth.
meek   souls   will   re - ceive   Him   still,   The   dear   Christ   en - ters   in.
come   to   us,   a - bide   with   us,   Our   Lord   Em - man - u - el!

RAINDROPS KEEP FALLIN' ON MY HEAD

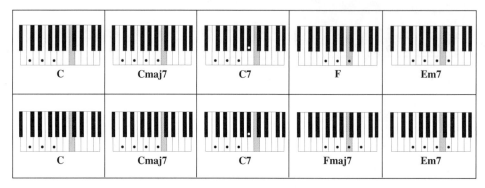

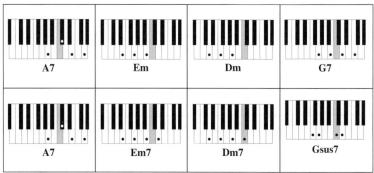

Lyric by HAL DAVID
Music by BURT BACHARACH

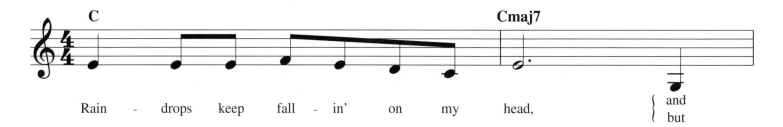

Rain - drops keep fall - in' on my head,   and / but

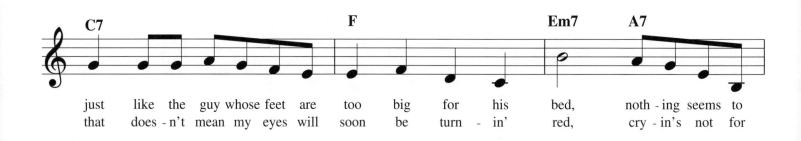

just like the guy whose feet are too big for his bed, noth-ing seems to
that does-n't mean my eyes will soon be turn-in' red, cry-in's not for

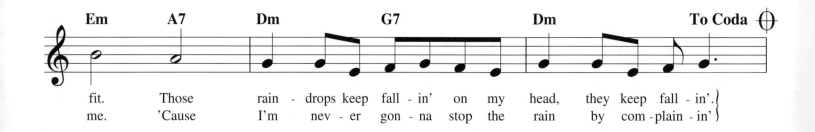

fit. Those rain - drops keep fall - in' on my head, they keep fall - in'.
me. 'Cause I'm nev - er gon - na stop the rain by com - plain - in'

So I just did me some talk - in' to the sun, and

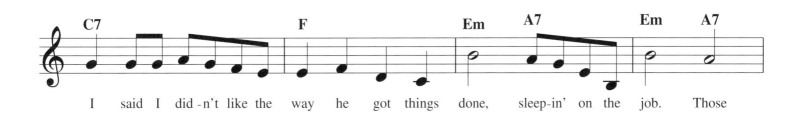

I said I did -n't like the way he got things done, sleep-in' on the job. Those

rain - drops are fall - in' on my head, they keep fall-in'! But there's one thing I know, ___

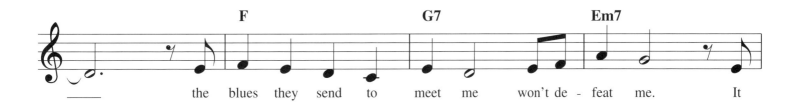

___ the blues they send to meet me won't de - feat me. It

D.C. al Coda

won't be long till hap - pi - ness steps up to greet me. _____

CODA

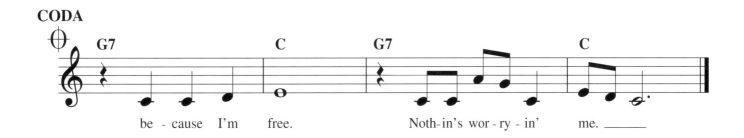

be - cause I'm free. Noth-in's wor - ry - in' me. _____

RIBBON IN THE SKY

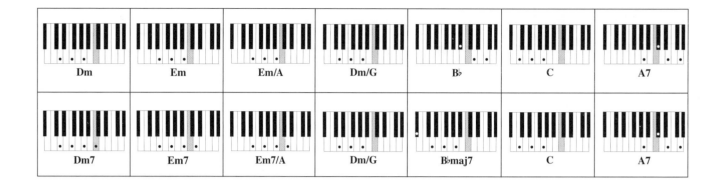

Words and Music by
STEVIE WONDER

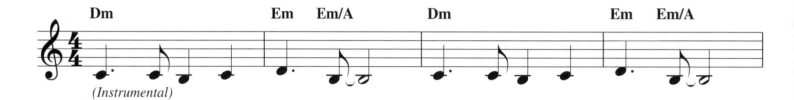

(Instrumental)

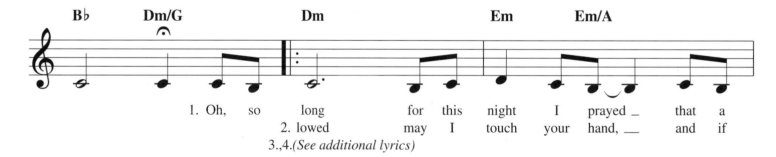

1. Oh, so long   for this night   I   prayed _   that a
2. lowed   may I   touch   your   hand, __   and if
3.,4.(See additional lyrics)

star   would   guide   you   my   way _____   to   share
pleased   may   I   once   a - gain, _____   so   that

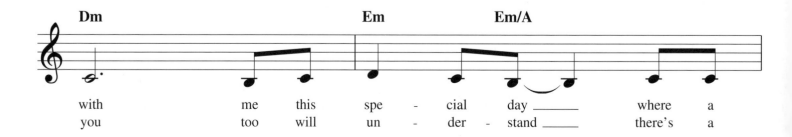

with   me   this   spe - cial   day _____   where   a
you   too   will   un - der - stand _____   there's a

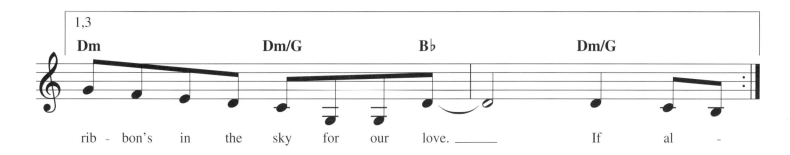

1,3

ribbon's in the sky for our love. _____ If al -

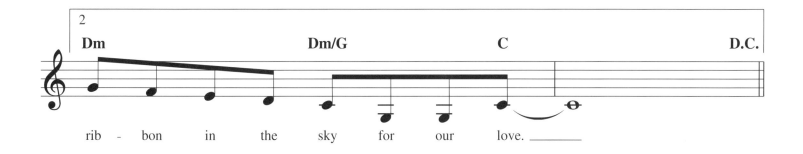

2

rib - bon in the sky for our love. _____

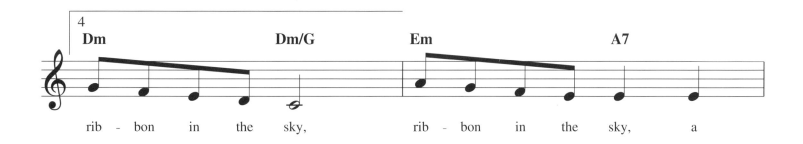

4

rib - bon in the sky, rib - bon in the sky, a

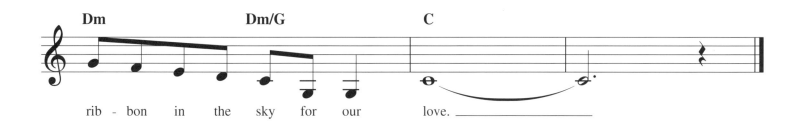

rib - bon in the sky for our love. _____

Additional Lyrics

3. This is not a coincidence,
   And far more than a lucky chance.
   But what is that is always meant
   Is our ribbon in the sky for our love.

4. We can't lose with God on our side.
   From now on it will be you and I
   And our ribbon in the sky, ribbon in the sky,
   A ribbon in the sky for our love.

RUDOLPH THE RED-NOSED REINDEER

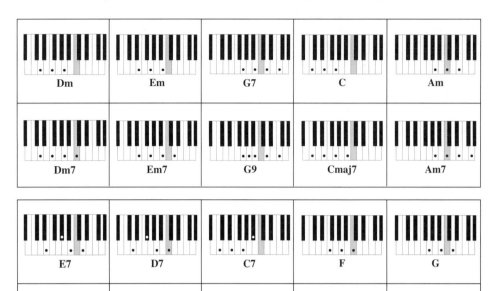

Music and Lyrics by
JOHNNY MARKS

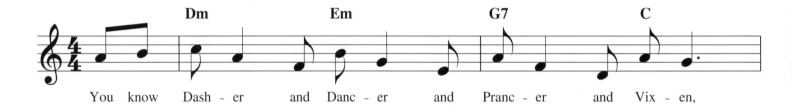

You know Dash - er and Danc - er and Pranc - er and Vix - en,

Com - et and Cu - pid and Don - ner and Blitz - en, but do you re -

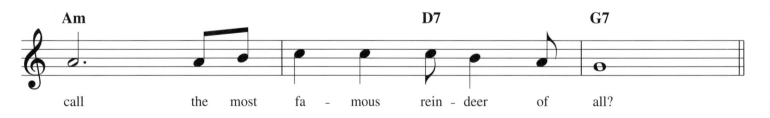

call the most fa - mous rein - deer of all?

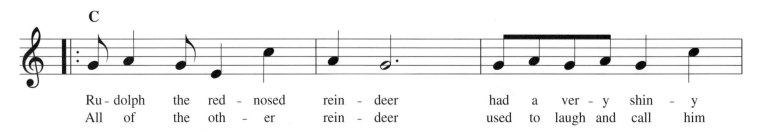

Ru - dolph the red - nosed rein - deer had a ver - y shin - y
All of the oth - er rein - deer used to laugh and call him

SATIN DOLL
from SOPHISTICATED LADIES

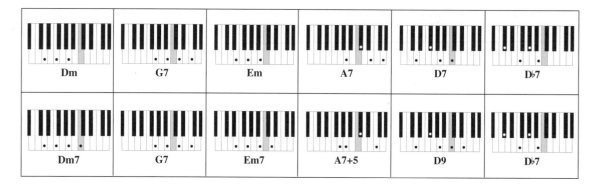

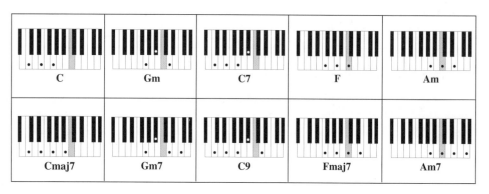

Words by JOHNNY MERCER and BILLY STRAYHORN
Music by DUKE ELLINGTON

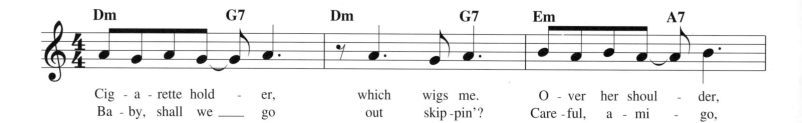

Cig - a - rette hold - er,   which wigs me.   O - ver her shoul - der,
Ba - by, shall we ___ go   out skip -pin'?   Care -ful, a - mi - go,

she digs me   Out cat - tin'   that sat - in
you're flip - pin'.   Speaks Lat - in,   that sat - in

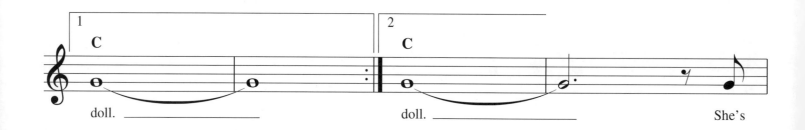

doll. _____   doll. _____   She's

no - bod - y's fool, ___ so I'm play - ing it cool ___ as can be. ___

_____ I'll give it a whirl, ___ but I ain't ___

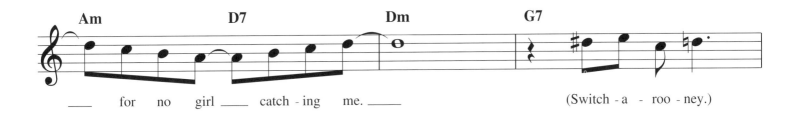

___ for no girl ___ catch -ing me. _____ (Switch -a - roo - ney.)

Tel - e - phone num - bers; well, you know,

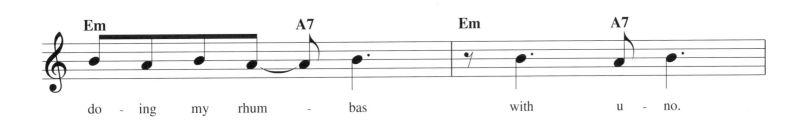

do - ing my rhum - bas with u - no.

And that 'n' my sat - in doll. _____

SAVING ALL MY LOVE FOR YOU

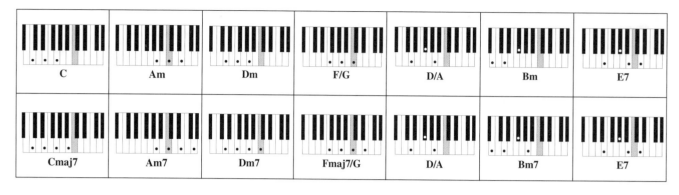

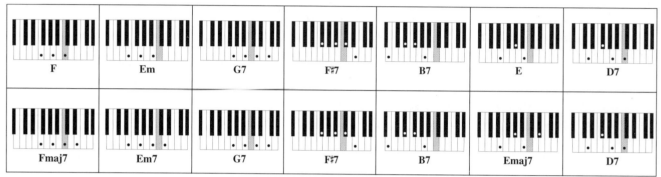

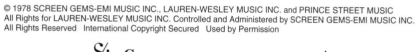

Words by GERRY GOFFIN
Music by MICHAEL MASSER

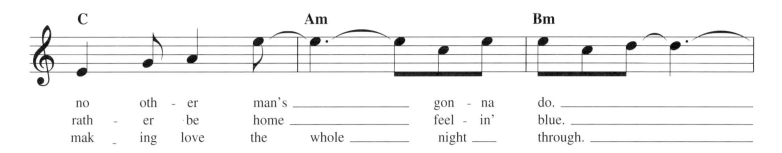

no oth - er man's _____ gon - na do. _____
rath - er be home _____ feel - in' blue. _____
mak - ing love the whole _____ night ___ through. _____

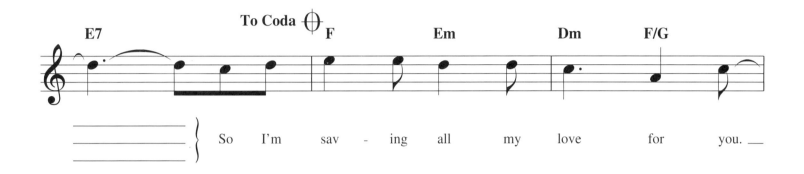

To Coda

_____ So I'm sav - ing all my love for you. ___

_____ *(Instrumental)* It's

_____ *(Instrumental)* You used to

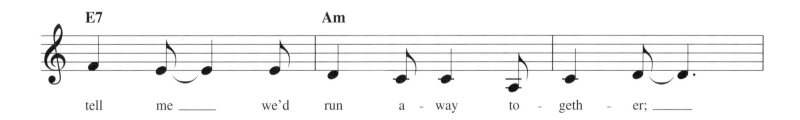

tell me _____ we'd run a - way to - geth - er; _____

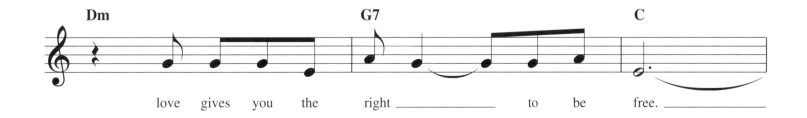

love gives you the right _____ to be free. _____

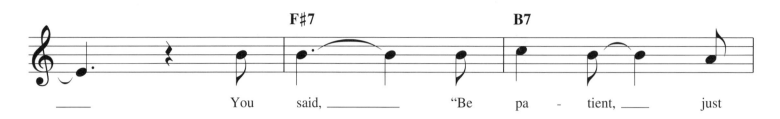

You said, _____ "Be pa - tient, ____ just

wait a lit - tle long - er," _____ but that's just ____ an

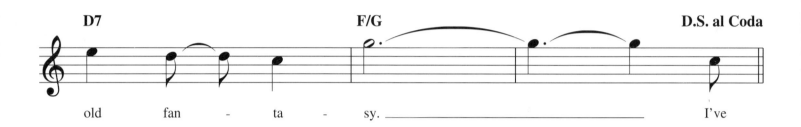

old fan - ta - sy. _____ I've

CODA

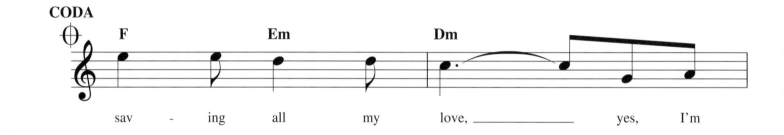

sav - ing all my love, _____ yes, I'm

sav - ing all my love, _____ yes, I'm sav - ing all my

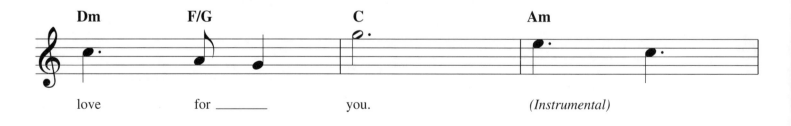

love for _____ you. *(Instrumental)*

No oth - er

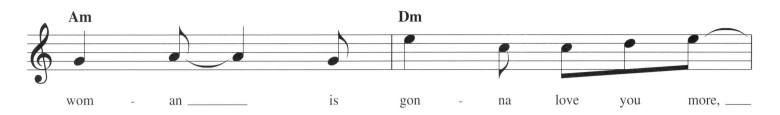

wom - an _____ is gon - na love you more, ____

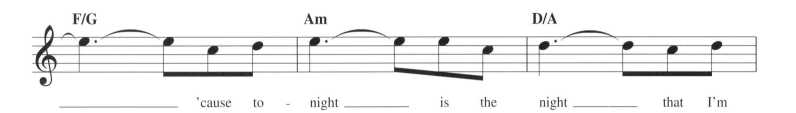

_____ 'cause to - night _____ is the night _____ that I'm

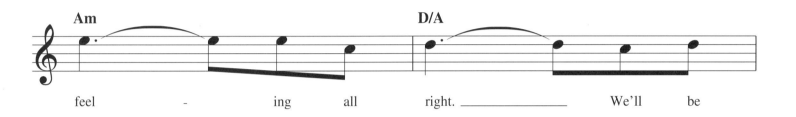

feel - ing all right. _____ We'll be

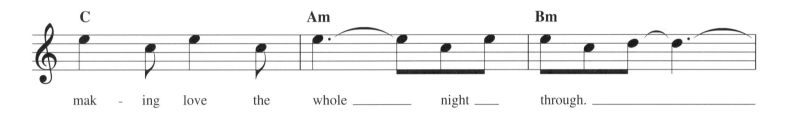

mak - ing love the whole _____ night ____ through. _____

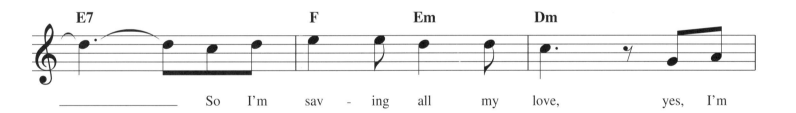

_____ So I'm sav - ing all my love, yes, I'm

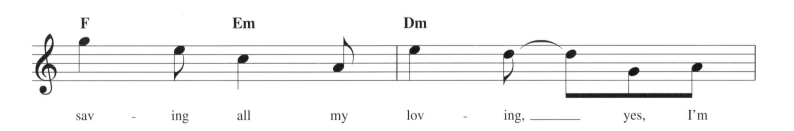

sav - ing all my lov - ing, _____ yes, I'm

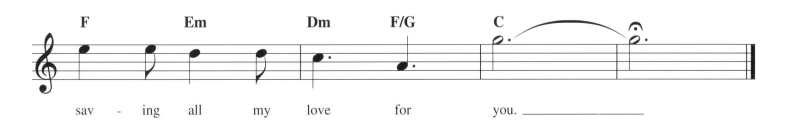

sav - ing all my love for you. _____

SENTIMENTAL JOURNEY

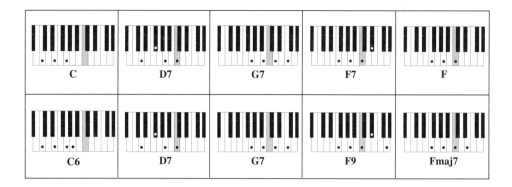

Words and Music by BUD GREEN,
LES BROWN and BEN HOMER

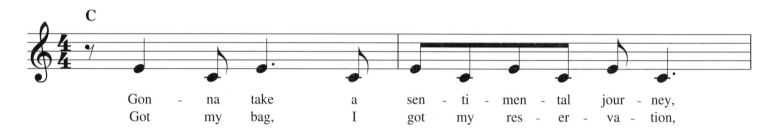

Gon - na take a sen - ti - men - tal jour - ney,
Got my bag, I got my res - er - va - tion,

gon - na set my heart at ease. _____
spent each dime I could af - ford. _____

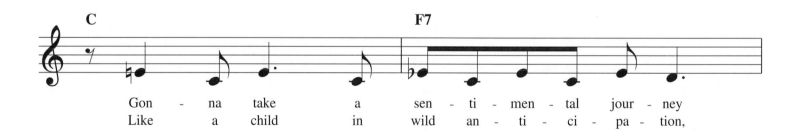

Gon - na take a sen - ti - men - tal jour - ney
Like a child in wild an - ti - ci - pa - tion,

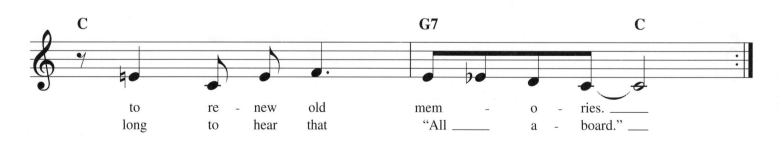

to re - new old mem - o - ries. _____
long to hear that "All _____ a - board." __

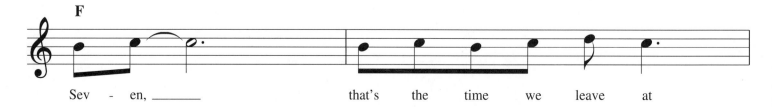

Sev - en, _____ that's the time we leave at

133

sev - en, _____ I'll be wait - in' up for

Heav - en, _____ count - in' ev - 'ry mile of

rail - road track _____ that takes me back. _____

Nev - er thought my heart could be so "yearn - y,"

why did I de - cide to roam? _____

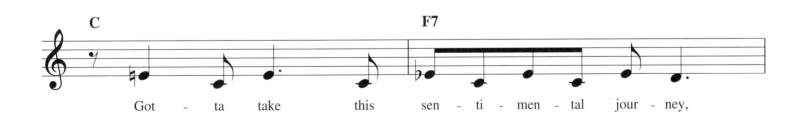

Got - ta take this sen - ti - men - tal jour - ney,

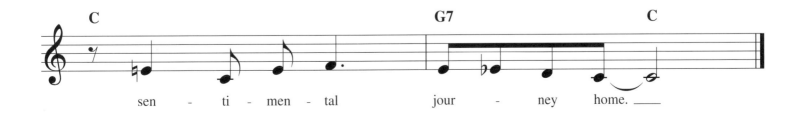

sen - ti - men - tal jour - ney home. _____

SILVER BELLS
from the Paramount Picture THE LEMON DROP KID

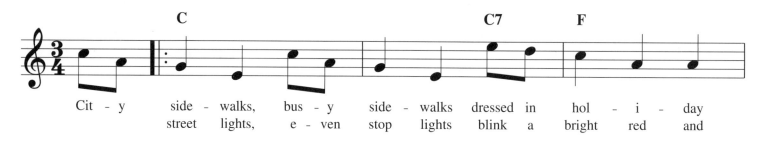

Words and Music by JAY LIVINGSTON
and RAY EVANS

Cit - y side - walks, bus - y side - walks dressed in hol - i - day
street lights, e - ven stop lights blink a bright red and

style in the air there's a feel - ing of Christ - mas._____ Chil-dren
green, as the shop - pers rush home with their treas - ures._____ Hear the

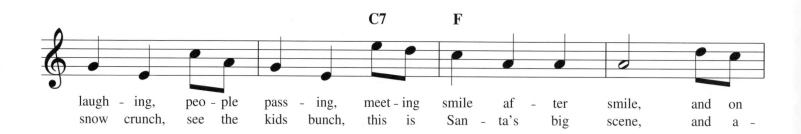

laugh - ing, peo - ple pass - ing, meet - ing smile af - ter smile, and on
snow crunch, see the kids bunch, this is San - ta's big scene, and a -

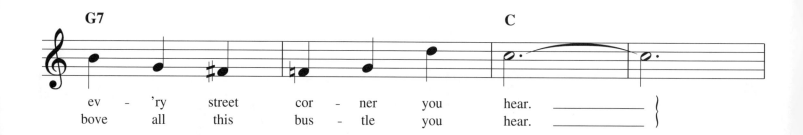

ev - 'ry street cor - ner you hear._____
bove all this bus - tle you hear._____

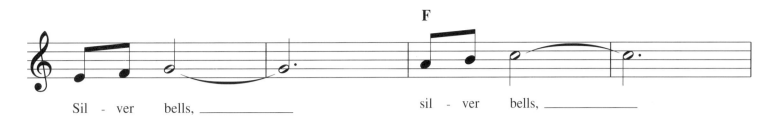

Sil - ver bells, _____ sil - ver bells, _____

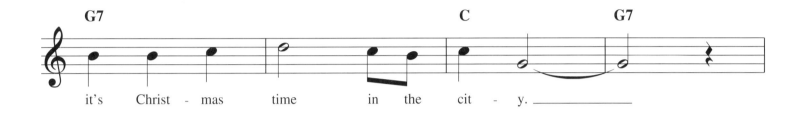

it's Christ - mas time in the cit - y. _____

Ring - a - ling, _____ hear them ring, _____

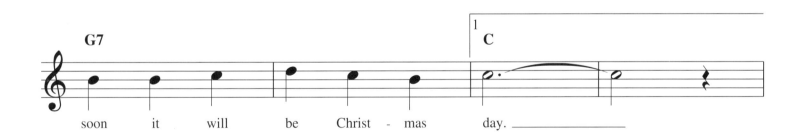

soon it will be Christ - mas day. _____

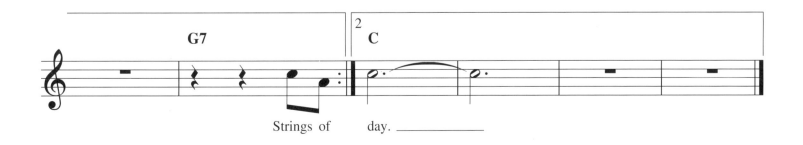

Strings of day. _____

SKYLARK

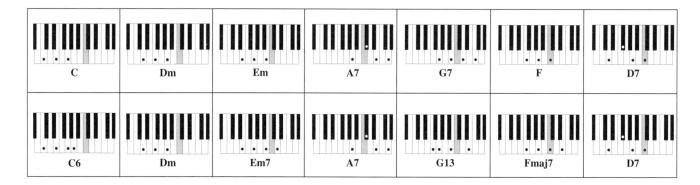

Words by JOHNNY MERCER
Music by HOAGY CARMICHAEL

Sky - lark _____ have you an - y - thing to
Sky - lark _____ have you seen a val - ley

say to me? _____ Won't you tell me where my love can be? _____
green with spring? _____ Where my heart can go a jour - ney - ing?

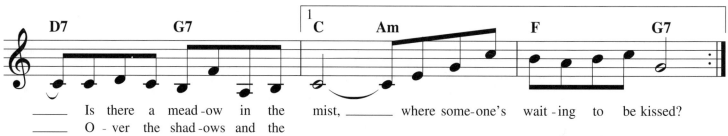

_____ Is there a mead - ow in the mist, _____ where some - one's wait - ing to be kissed?
_____ O - ver the shad - ows and the

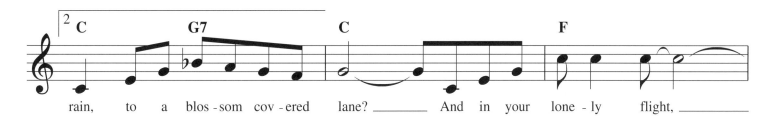

rain, to a blos-som cov-ered lane? _____ And in your lone-ly flight, _____

_____ have-n't you heard the mu - sic in the night. _____ Won-der-ful mu - sic,

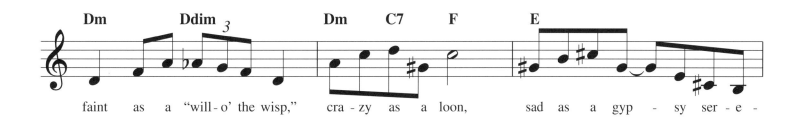

faint as a "will-o' the wisp," cra-zy as a loon, sad as a gyp - sy ser-e -

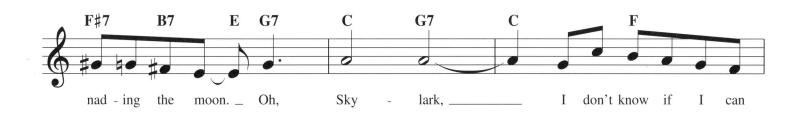

nad-ing the moon._ Oh, Sky - lark, _____ I don't know if I can

find these things. _____ But my heart is rid-ing on your wings, _____

_____ so, if you see them an-y-where won't you lead me there?

SMOKE GETS IN YOUR EYES
from ROBERTA

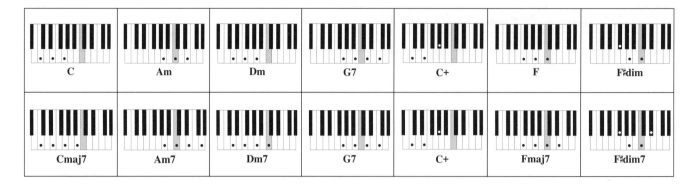

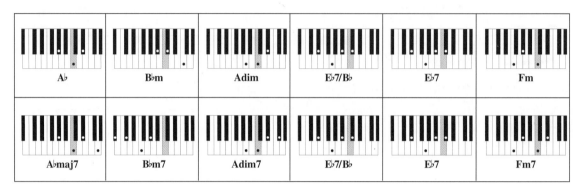

Words by OTTO HARBACH
Music by JEROME KERN

So I chaffed _____ them and I gay - ly laughed _____ to think they could

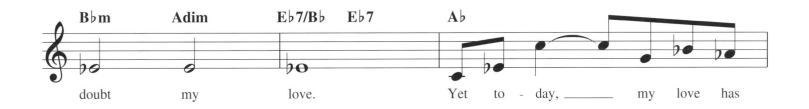

doubt my love. Yet to - day, _____ my love has

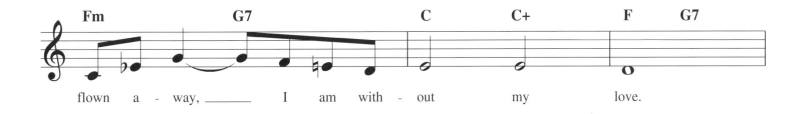

flown a - way, _____ I am with - out my love.

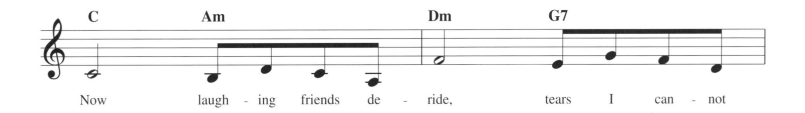

Now laugh - ing friends de - ride, tears I can - not

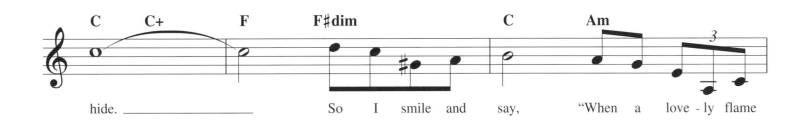

hide. _____ So I smile and say, "When a love - ly flame

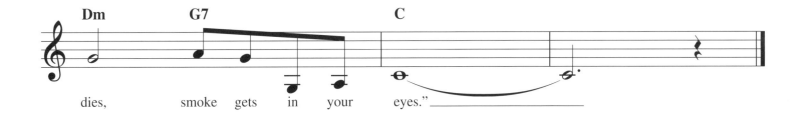

dies, smoke gets in your eyes." _____

SOLITUDE

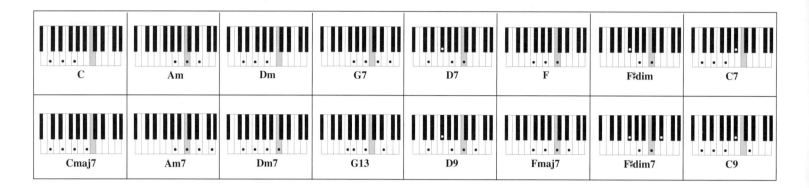

Words and Music by DUKE ELLINGTON,
EDDIE DE LANGE and IRVING MILLS

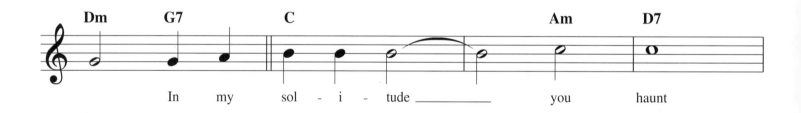

In my sol - i - tude _____ you haunt

me with rev - er - ies _____ of days gone by. _____

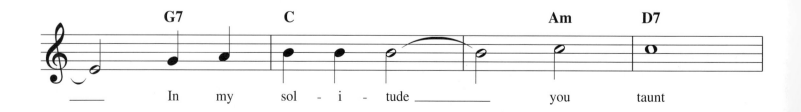

_____ In my sol - i - tude _____ you taunt

me with mem - o - ries _____ that nev - er die. _____

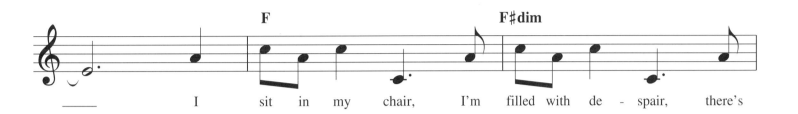

_____ I sit in my chair, I'm filled with de - spair, there's

no one could be so sad. With gloom ev - 'ry - where, I

sit and I stare. I know that I'll soon go mad. In my

sol - i - tude _____ I'm pray - ing dear

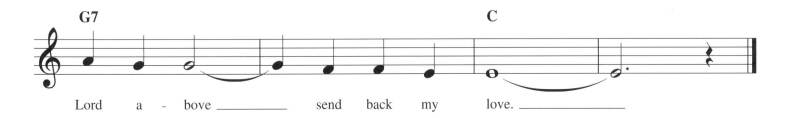

Lord a - bove _____ send back my love. _____

SOMEWHERE OUT THERE
from AN AMERICAN TAIL

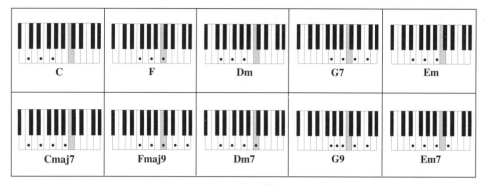

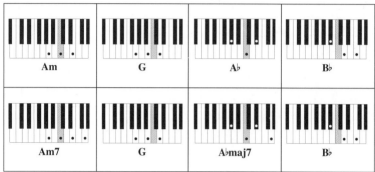

Words and Music by JAMES HORNER,
BARRY MANN and CYNTHIA WEIL

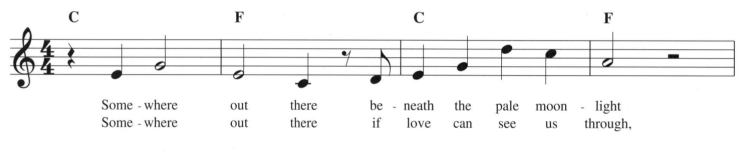

Some - where   out   there   be - neath   the   pale   moon - light
Some - where   out   there   if   love   can   see   us   through,

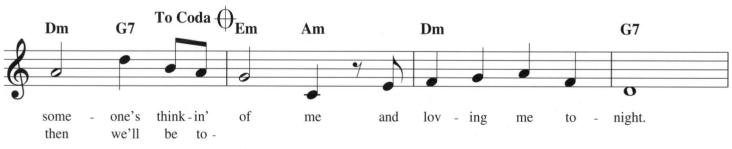

some - one's   think - in'   of   me   and   lov - ing   me   to - night.
then   we'll   be   to -

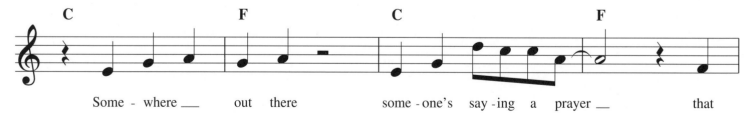

Some - where ___   out   there   some - one's   say - ing   a   prayer ___   that

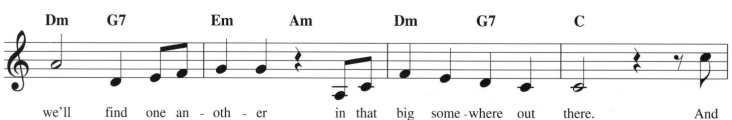

we'll   find   one   an - oth - er   in   that   big   some - where   out   there.   And

e - ven though I know how ver - y far a - part we are, it

helps to think we might be wish - in' on the same bright star. And

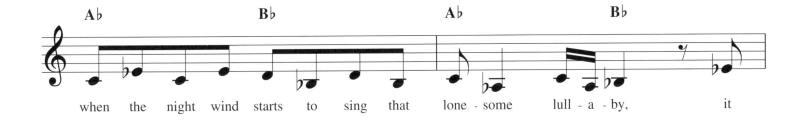

when the night wind starts to sing that lone - some lull - a - by, it

helps to think we're sleep - ing un - der - neath the same big sky.

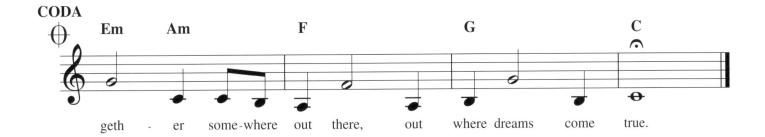

geth - er some-where out there, out where dreams come true.

SOPHISTICATED LADY
from SOPHISTICATED LADIES

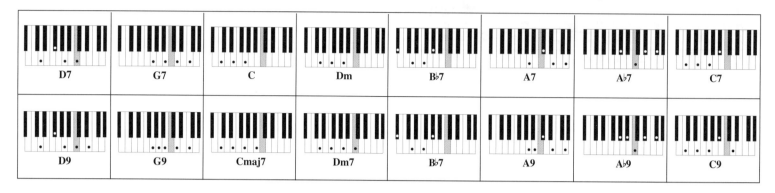

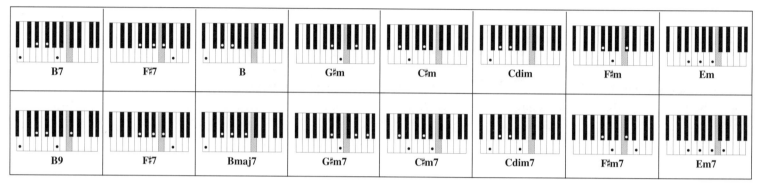

Words and Music by DUKE ELLINGTON,
IRVING MILLS and MITCHELL PARISH

fools   in   love   soon grow wise. _____ The years have changed you, some-how;   I

see you now...   Smok - ing, drink - ing, nev - er think - ing of   to -

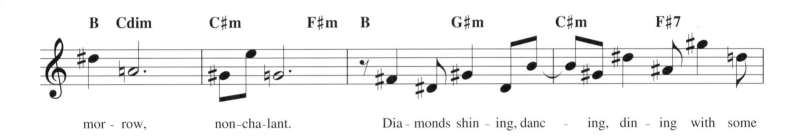
mor - row,   non-cha-lant.   Dia - monds shin - ing, danc - ing, din - ing with some

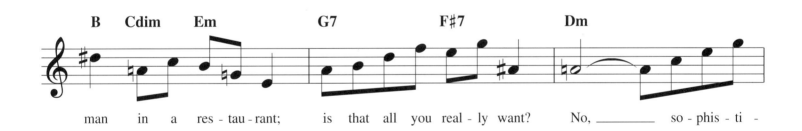
man   in a res - tau - rant;   is   that all you real - ly want?   No, _____ so - phis - ti -

cat - ed la - dy, I   know, _____ you miss the   love   you   lost   long a -

go, _____ and when no - bod - y is nigh   you   cry. _____

STAND BY ME

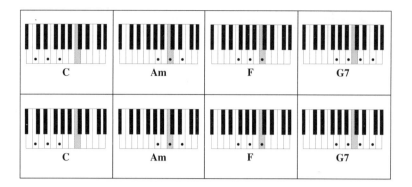

Words and Music by JERRY LEIBER,
MIKE STOLLER and BEN E. KING

stand _____ by me, oh, stand, _____ stand by me,

stand by me. _____ If the sea _____ that we look up - on

should tum - ble and fall, or the moun - tain _____ should

crum - ble _____ in the sea, I won't cry, I won't

cry, no _____ I _____ won't shed a tear just as

long _____ as you stand, _____ stand by me. So, dar - ling, dar - ling,

STARDUST

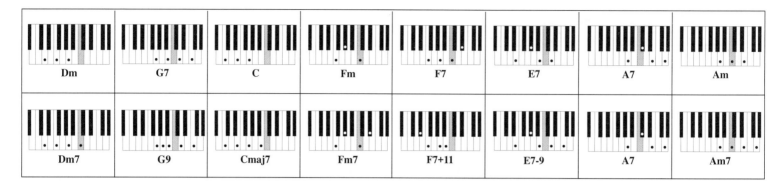

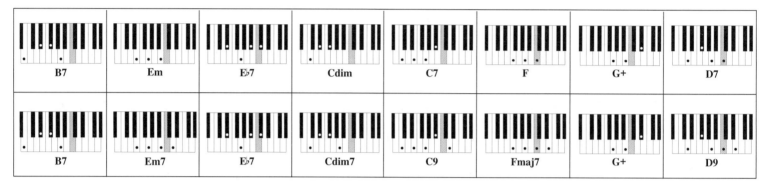

Words by MITCHELL PARISH
Music by HOAGY CARMICHAEL

STELLA BY STARLIGHT
from the Paramount Picture THE UNINVITED

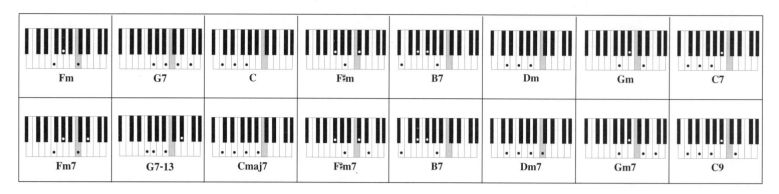

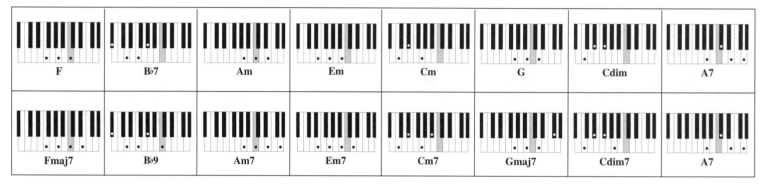

Words by NED WASHINGTON
Music by VICTOR YOUNG

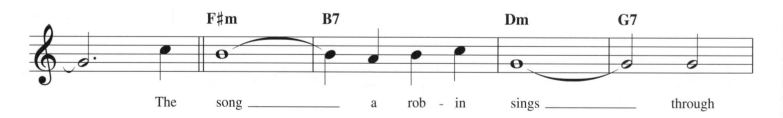

The song _____ a rob - in sings _____ through

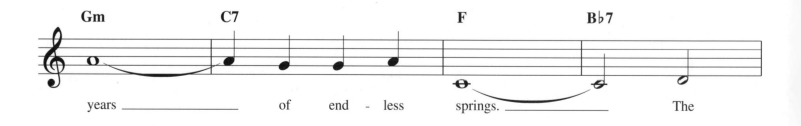

years _____ of end - less springs. _____ The

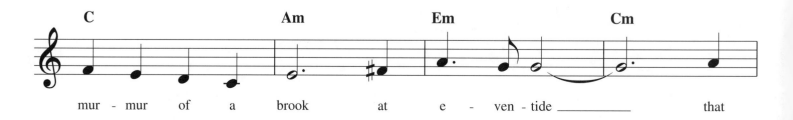

mur - mur of a brook at e - ven - tide _____ that

151

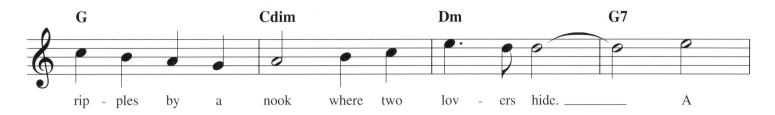

rip - ples by a nook where two lov - ers hide. _____ A

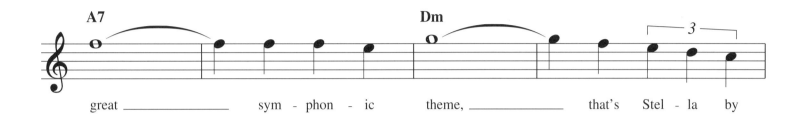

great _____ sym - phon - ic theme, _____ that's Stel - la by

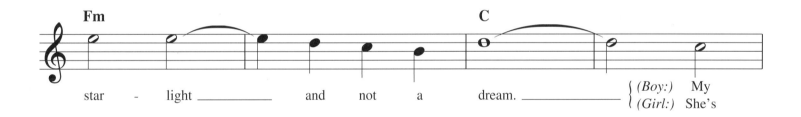

star - light _____ and not a dream. _____ { (Boy:) My
{ (Girl:) She's

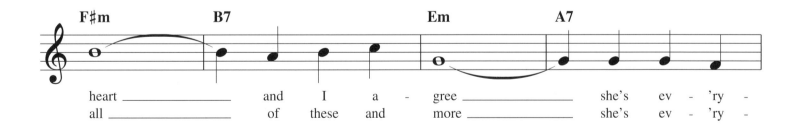

heart _____ and I a - gree _____ she's ev - 'ry -
all _____ of these and more _____ she's ev - 'ry -

thing _____ on earth to me. _____
thing _____ that you'd a - dore. _____

STORMY WEATHER
(Keeps Rainin' All the Time)

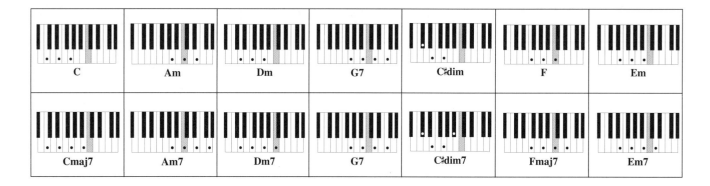

Lyric by TED KOEHLER
Music by HAROLD ARLEN

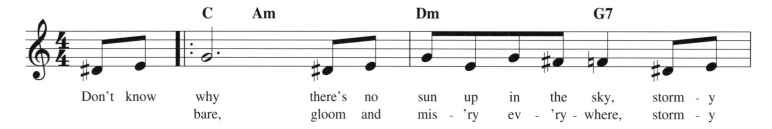

Don't know why there's no sun up in the sky, storm-y
bare, gloom and mis-'ry ev-'ry-where, storm-y

weath-er. _____ Since my man and I ain't to-geth-er, _____
weath-er. _____ Just can't get my poor self to-geth-er. _____

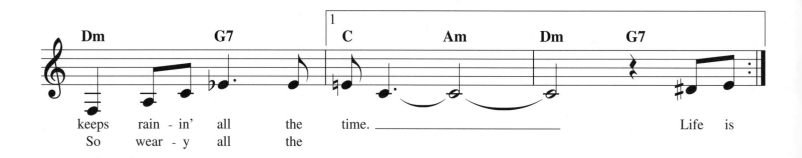

keeps rain-in' all the time. _____ Life is
So wear-y all the

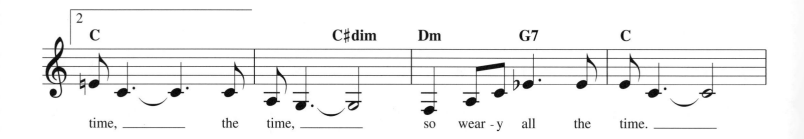

time, _____ the time, _____ so wear-y all the time. _____

When he went a - way the blues walked in   and met me.   If he stays a - way old rock -in'

chair   will   get   me.   All   I   do   is   pray   the Lord   a - bove   will   let   me

walk   in   the   sun   once   more.   Can't go   on,   ev -'ry - thing I had is gone, storm -y

weath-er._____   Since my man and I   ain't to - geth - er,_____   keeps rain-in' all   the

time _____   keeps rain - in' all   the   time. _____

TANGERINE
from the Paramount Picture THE FLEET'S IN

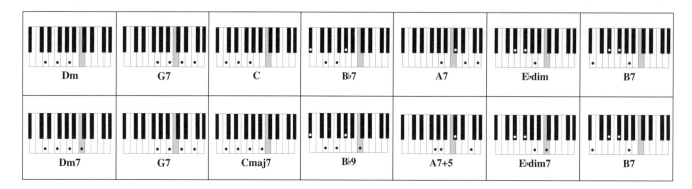

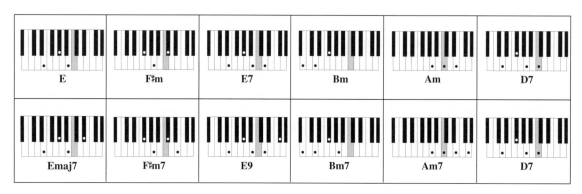

Words by JOHNNY MERCER
Music by VICTOR SCHERTZINGER

Tan - ger -

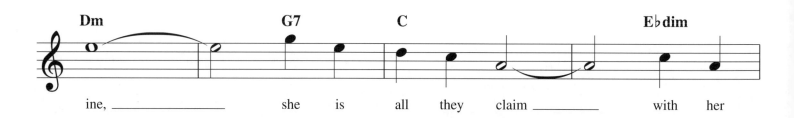

ine, _____ she is all they claim _____ with her

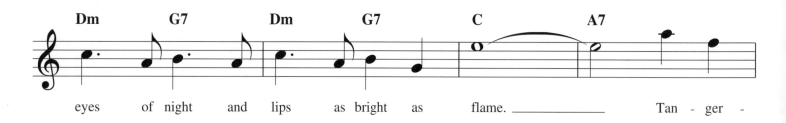

eyes of night and lips as bright as flame. _____ Tan - ger -

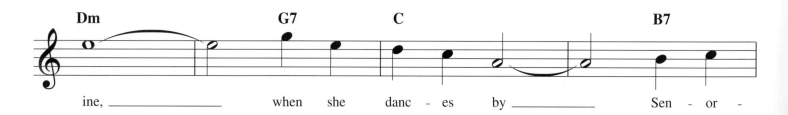

ine, _____ when she danc - es by _____ Sen - or -

i - tas stare and ca - bal - le - ros sigh. _____ And I've

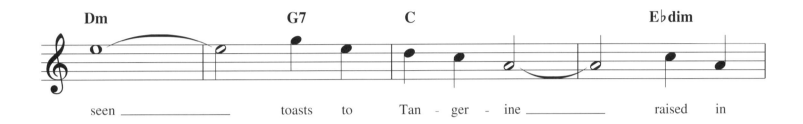

seen _____ toasts to Tan - ger - ine _____ raised in

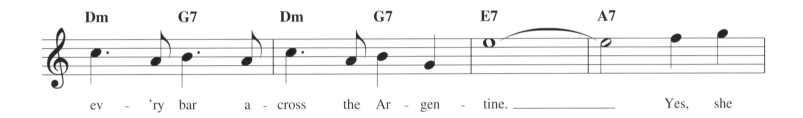

ev - 'ry bar a - cross the Ar - gen - tine. _____ Yes, she

has them all on the run but her heart be - longs to just one. Her

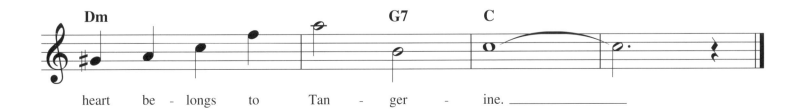

heart be - longs to Tan - ger - ine. _____

TEARS IN HEAVEN

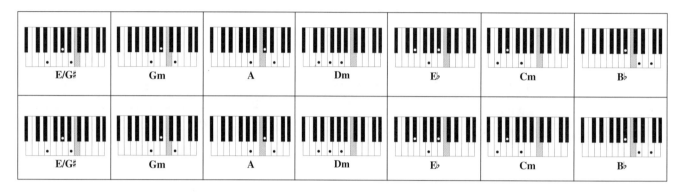

Words and Music by ERIC CLAPTON
and WILL JENNINGS

Would you know   my   name _____   if   I   saw you   in   heav-
Would you hold   my   hand _____   if   I   saw you   in   heav-
Would you know   my   name _____   if   I   saw you   in   heav-

en?   Would it   be   the   same _____   if   I   saw you   in   heav-
en?   Would you help   me   stand _____   if   I   saw you   in   heav-
en?   Would you   be   the   same _____   if   I   saw you   in   heav-

en?   (1., 3.) I   must   be   strong __   and   car-ry   on __
en?   (2.) I'll   find   my   way ___   through night   and   day _
en?

'cause I know ___ I don't be-long ____ here in heav-en. *(Instrumental)*
'cause I know ___ I just can't stay ____ here in heav-en.

Time can bring you down, ___ time can bend your knees. __ *(Instrumental)*

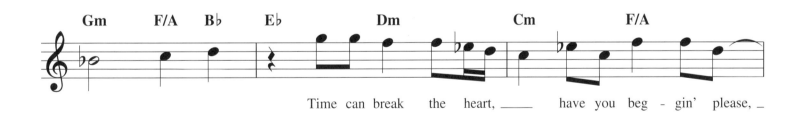

Time can break the heart, ___ have you beg-gin' please, _

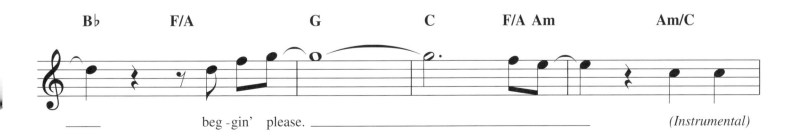

___ beg-gin' please. _____ *(Instrumental)*

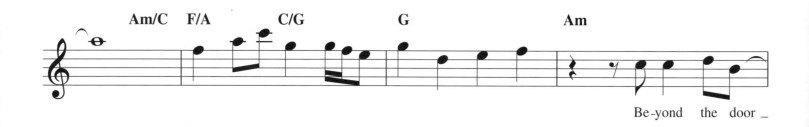

Be-yond the door _

_ there's peace, I'm sure, _ and I know _

_ there'll be no more _ tears in heav - en. *(Instrumental)*

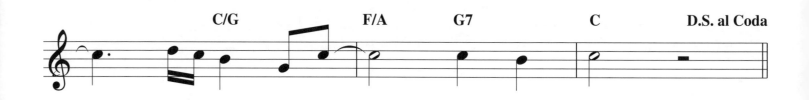

en. *(Instrumental)*

SILENT NIGHT

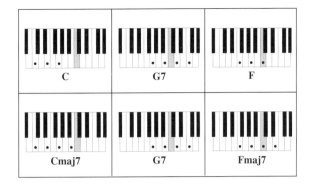

Words by JOSEPH MOHR
Translated by JOHN F. YOUNG
Music by FRANZ X. GRUBER

TILL THERE WAS YOU
from Meredith Willson's THE MUSIC MAN

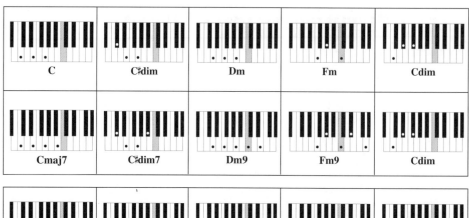

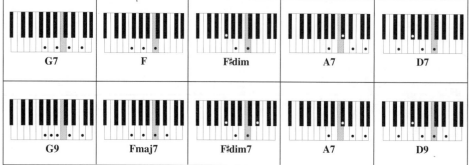

By MEREDITH WILLSON

There were bells on the hill, but I
birds in the sky, but I

nev - er heard them ring - ing. No, I nev - er heard them at
nev - er saw them wing - ing. No, I nev - er saw them at

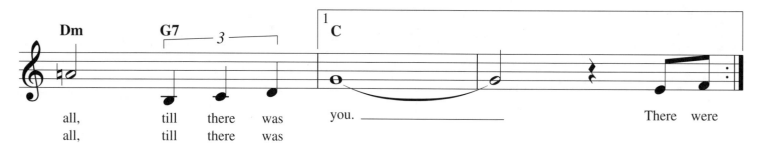

all, till there was you. _____ There were
all, till there was

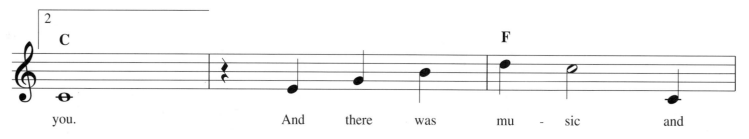

you. And there was mu - sic and

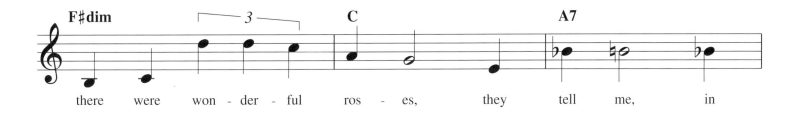

there were won - der - ful ros - es, they tell me, in

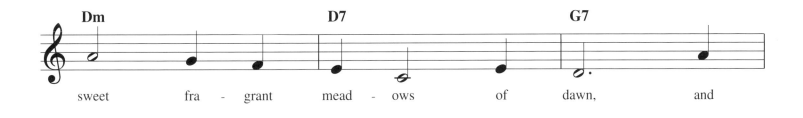

sweet fra - grant mead - ows of dawn, and

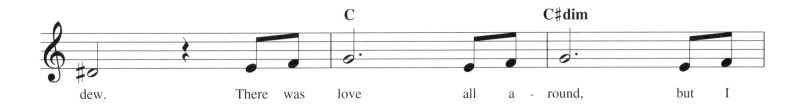

dew. There was love all a - round, but I

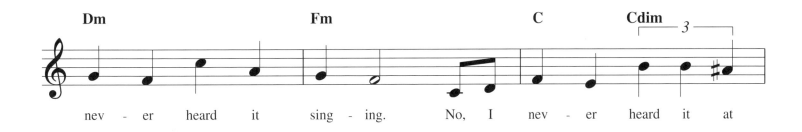

nev - er heard it sing - ing. No, I nev - er heard it at

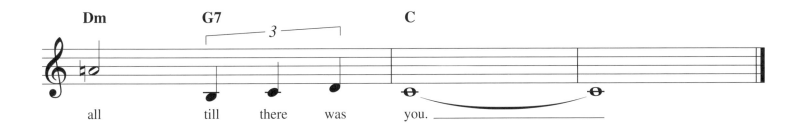

all till there was you.

TRY TO REMEMBER
from THE FANTASTICS

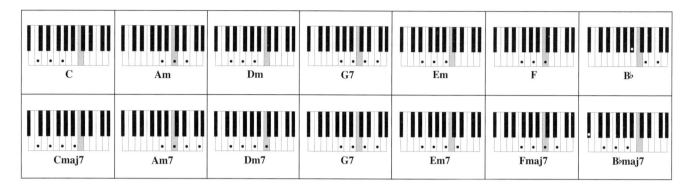

Words by TOM JONES
Music by HARVEY SCHMIDT

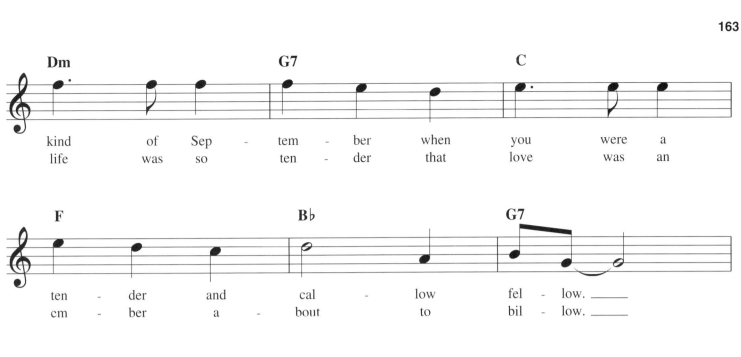

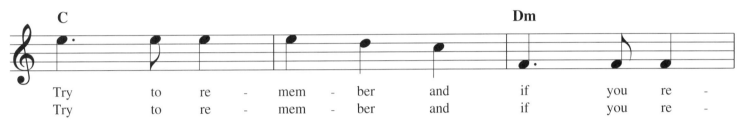

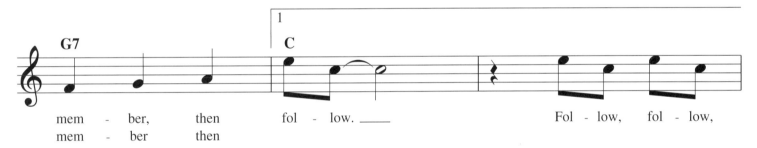

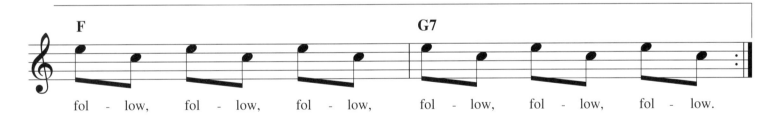

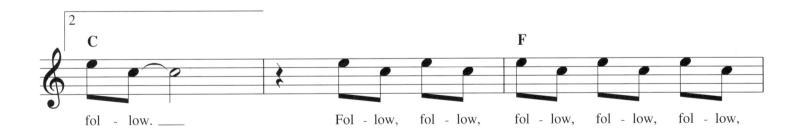

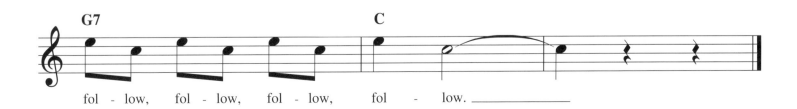

TWIST AND SHOUT

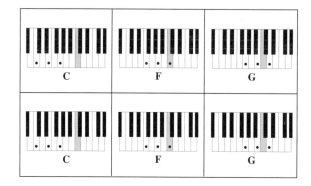

Words and Music by BERT RUSSELL
and PHIL MEDLEY

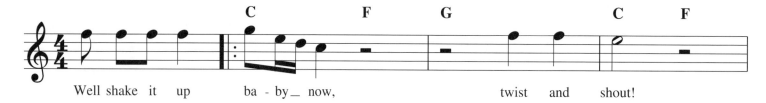

Well shake it up ba-by_ now,   twist and shout!

Come on, come on, come on, ba-by_ now,   Come on and work it on out. ___

Well, work it on out, ___   You know you look so good; ___
You know you twist, lit-tle girl, ___   You know you twist so fine ___

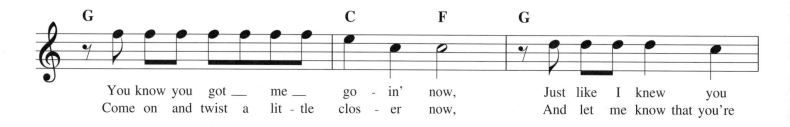

You know you got ___ me ___ go-in' now,   Just like I knew you
Come on and twist a lit-tle clos-er now,   And let me know that you're

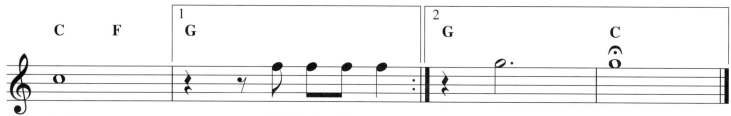

would.
mine.   Well shake it up   Ooo!

WHEN THE SAINTS GO MARCHING IN

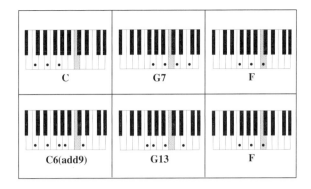

Words by KATHERINE E. PURVIS
Music by JAMES M. BLACK

WALTZ FOR DEBBY

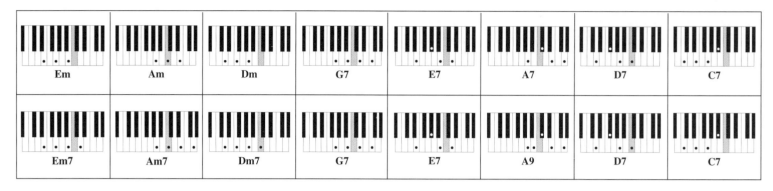

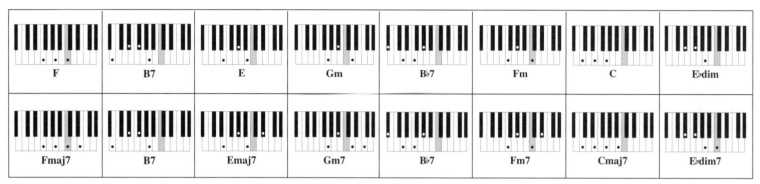

Lyric by GENE LEES
Music by BILL EVANS

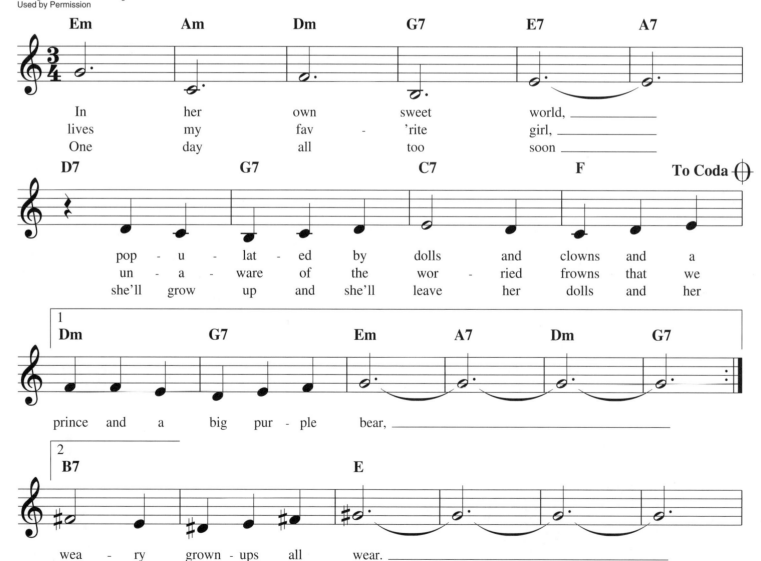

THE WAY WE WERE
from the Motion Picture THE WAY WE WERE

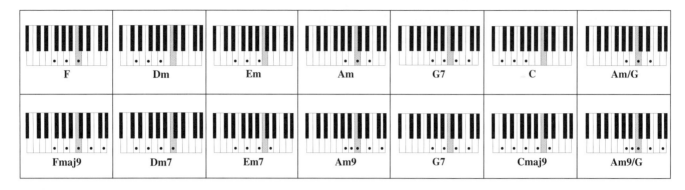

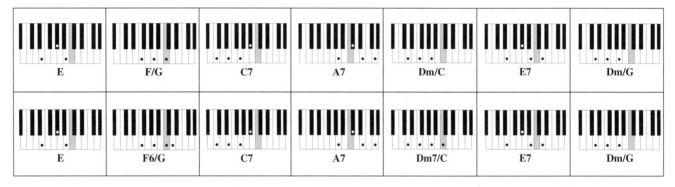

Words by ALAN and MARILYN BERGMAN
Music by MARVIN HAMLISCH

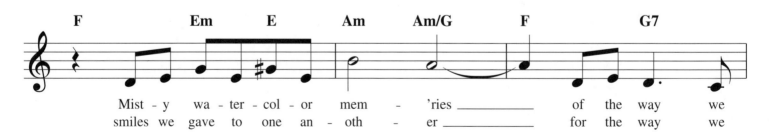

Mem - 'ries _____ light the cor - ners of my mind.
pic - tures _____ of the smiles we left be - hind,

Mist - y wa - ter - col - or mem - 'ries _____ of the way we
smiles we gave to one an - oth - er _____ for the way we

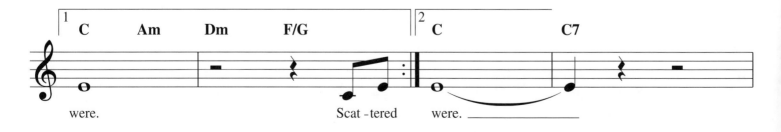

were.

Scat - tered were. _____

Can it be that it was all so sim - ple then, or has time re - writ - ten ev - 'ry

line? If we had the chance to do it all a - gain, tell me would we? ___

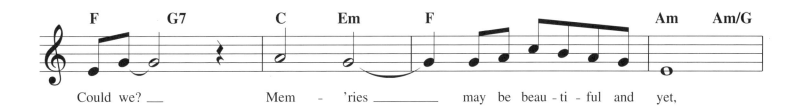

Could we? ___ Mem - 'ries _____ may be beau - ti - ful and yet,

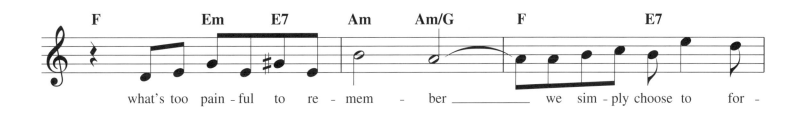

what's too pain - ful to re - mem - ber _____ we sim - ply choose to for -

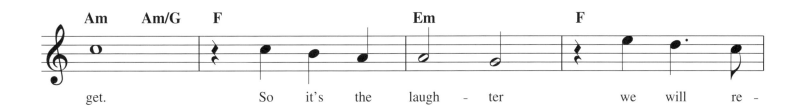

get. So it's the laugh - ter we will re -

mem - ber, _____ when - ev - er we re - mem - ber _____ the way we

were; the way we were. _____

THE WAY YOU LOOK TONIGHT
from SWING TIME

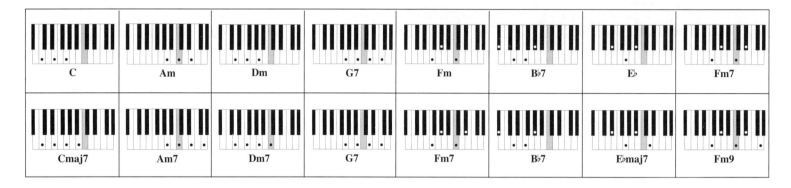

Words by DOROTHY FIELDS
Music by JEROME KERN

Some - day ~ when I'm aw - f'ly low,
love - ly, ~ with your smile so warm
Love - ly, ~ nev - er, nev - er change,

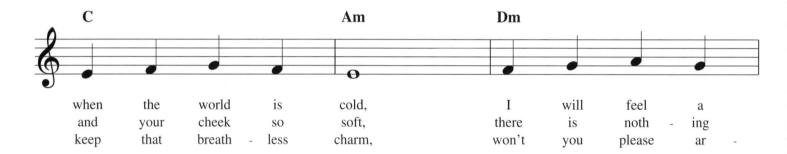

when the world is cold, ~ I will feel a
and your cheek so soft, ~ there is noth - ing
keep that breath - less charm, ~ won't you please ar -

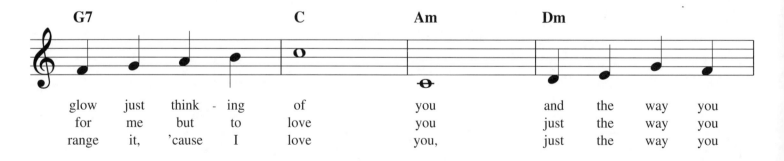

glow just think - ing of ~ you ~ and the way you
for me but to love ~ you ~ just the way you
range it, 'cause I love ~ you, ~ just the way you

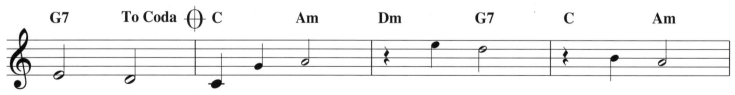

look to - night. *(Instrumental)*
look to - night.
look to -

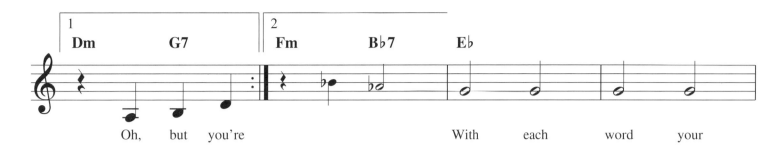

Oh, but you're

With each word your

ten - der - ness grows, _____ tear - ing my fear _____ a -

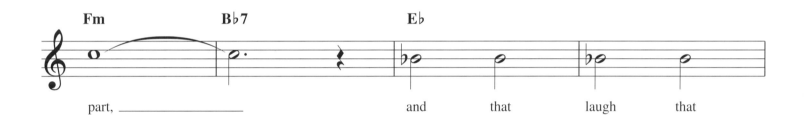

part, _____ and that laugh that

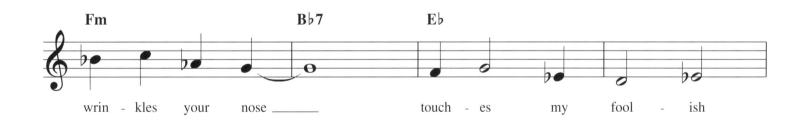

wrin - kles your nose _____ touch - es my fool - ish

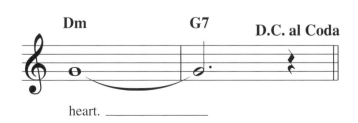

heart. _____

night. _____

WHAT A WONDERFUL WORLD

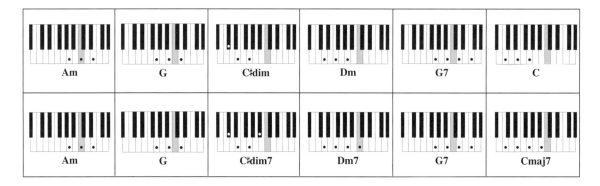

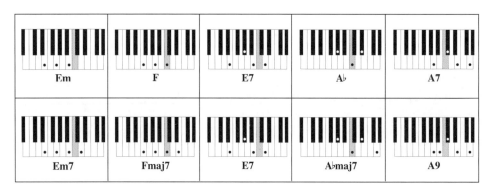

Words and Music by GEORGE DAVID WEISS
and BOB THIELE

I see trees of green,   red ros - es too,

I see them bloom   for me and you, ___ and I think ___ to my-self

what a won - der - ful   world. _____   I see skies of blue and

clouds   of white,   the   bright ___ bless-ed   day,   the   dark ___ sa-cred   night, ___ and I

WHEN I FALL IN LOVE
from ONE MINUTE TO ZERO

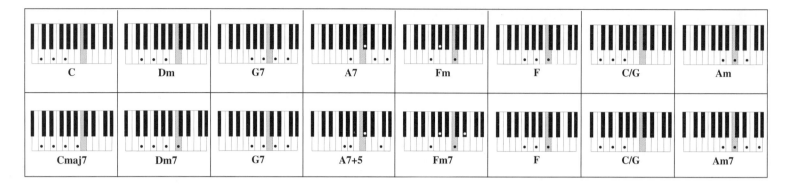

Words by EDWARD HEYMAN
Music by VICTOR YOUNG

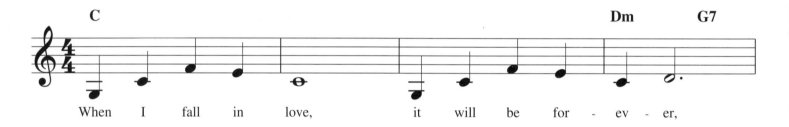

When I fall in love, it will be for-ev-er,

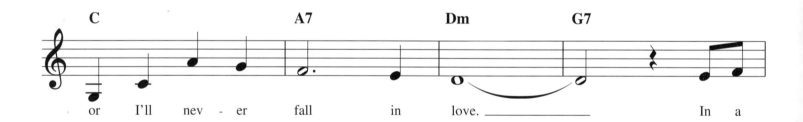

or I'll nev-er fall in love. _____ In a

rest-less world like this is, love is end-ed be-fore it's be-

gun. And too man-y moon-light kiss-es seem to

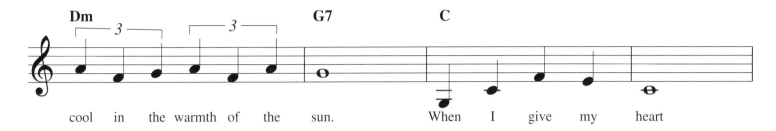

cool in the warmth of the sun. When I give my heart

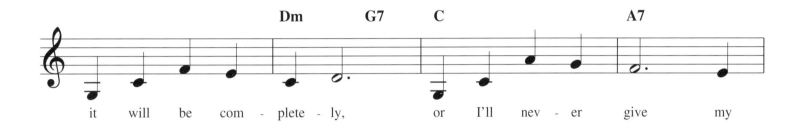

it will be com - plete - ly, or I'll nev - er give my

heart. _____ And the mo - ment I can

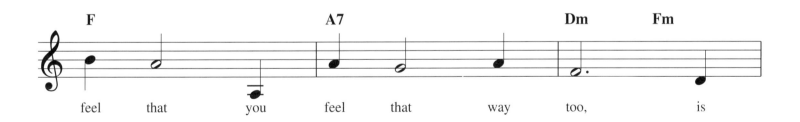

feel that you feel that way too, is

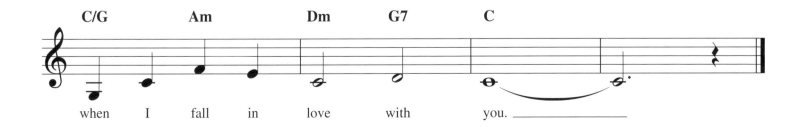

when I fall in love with you. _____

WONDERFUL TONIGHT

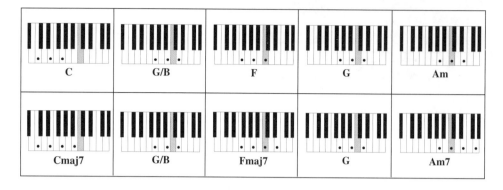

Words and Music by
ERIC CLAPTON

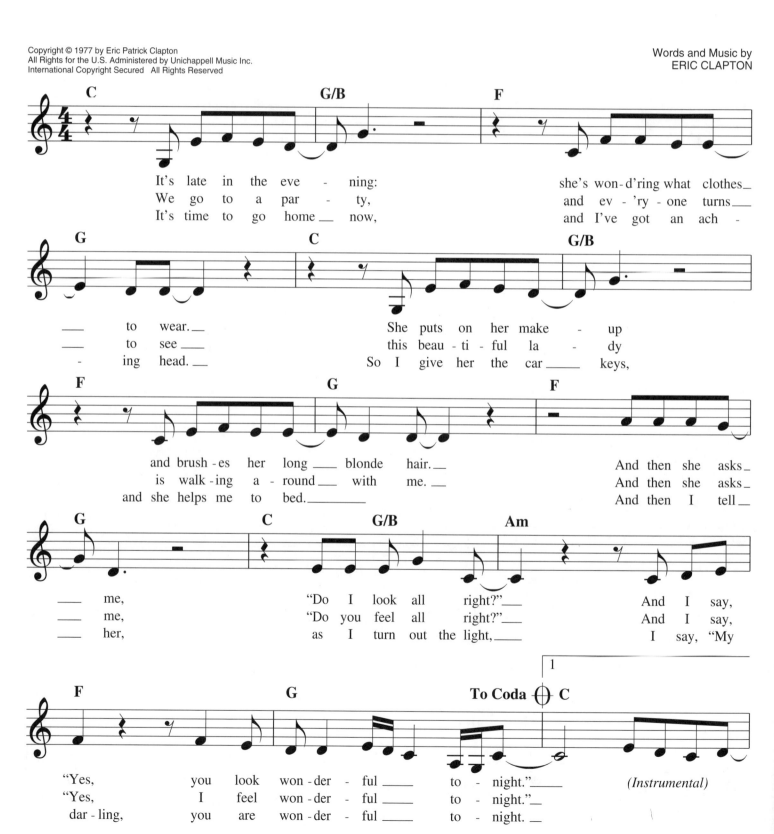

YOU'VE GOT A FRIEND

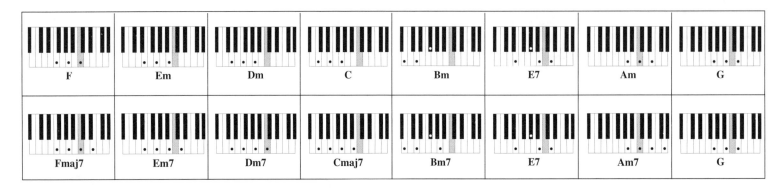

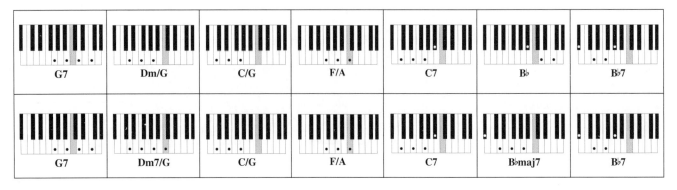

Words and Music by
CAROLE KING

When you're down _____ and trou - bled, and you need _
_____ a - bove _____ you grows _ dark _

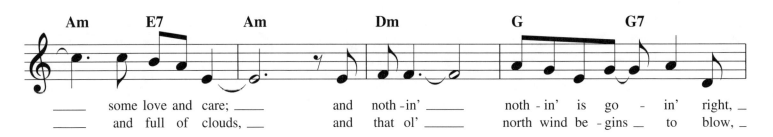

_____ some love and care; _____ and noth -in' _____ noth -in' is go - in' right, _
_____ and full of clouds, _ and that ol' _____ north wind be - gins _ to blow, _

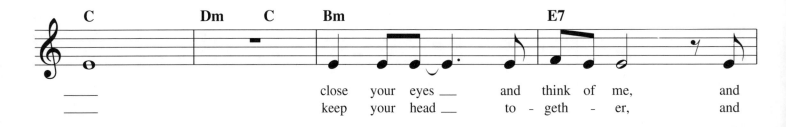

close your eyes _ and think of me, and
keep your head _ to - geth - er, and

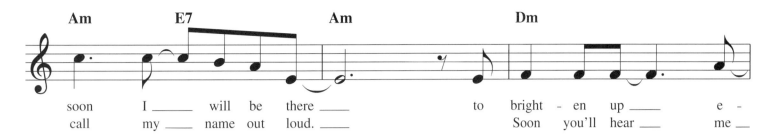

soon I _____ will be there _____ to bright - en up _____ e -
call my _____ name out loud. _____ Soon you'll hear _____ me _____

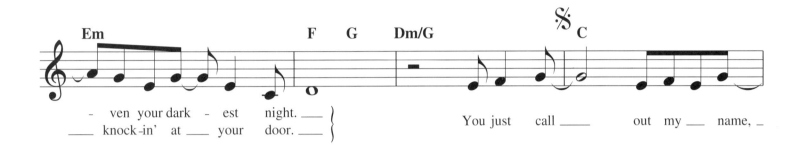

- ven your dark - est night. _____ } You just call _____ out my _ name, _
_____ knock-in' at _____ your door. _____ }

_____ and you know _____ wher-ev-er I am _____ I'll come run - nin' _____

to see you a - gain. _____ Win - ter, spring, sum-mer or fall, _

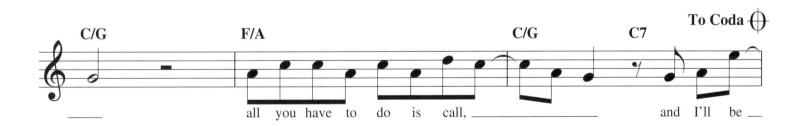

_____ all you have to do is call, _____ and I'll be _

_____ there. _____ You've got a friend. _____ If the sky _

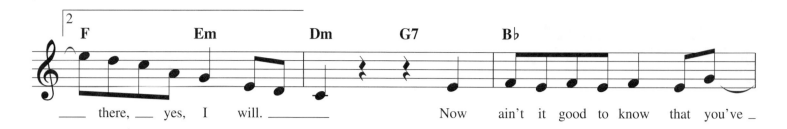

2

F ___ there, ___ yes, I will. _____ **Em** **Dm** **G7** Now ain't it good to know that you've ___ **B♭**

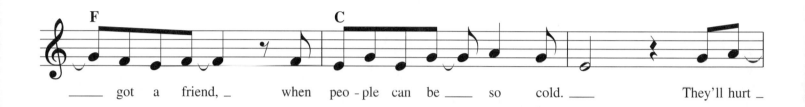

F ___ got a friend, ___ **C** when peo-ple can be ___ so cold. ___ They'll hurt ___

F ___ you, yes, and de-sert ___ you, **B♭7** and take your soul ___ if you let **Am**

D7 them. **Dm** Oh, but don't you let ___ them. **G** You just call ___ **D.S. al Coda**

CODA

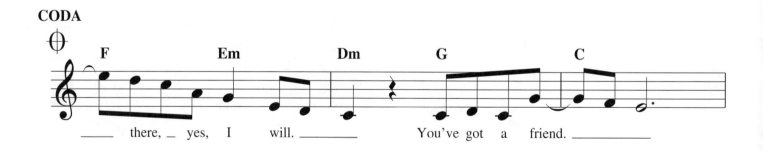

F ___ there, ___ yes, I will. _____ **Em** **Dm** **G** You've got a friend. _____ **C**

G7 You've got a friend. ___ **C** Ain't it good ___ to know you've got a **F** **Repeat and Fade**

YESTERDAY

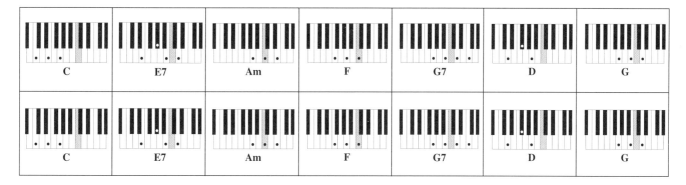

Words and Music by JOHN LENNON
and PAUL McCARTNEY

YOUR CHEATIN' HEART

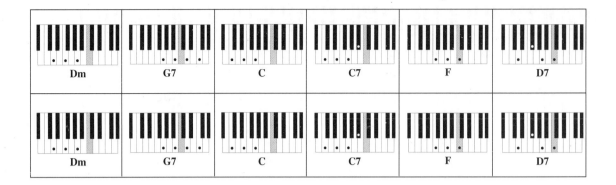

Words and Music by
HANK WILLIAMS

Your   cheat - in' ____

heart _____ will   make   you   weep _____ you'll   cry   and ____
heart _____ will   pine   some - day _____ and   crave   the ____

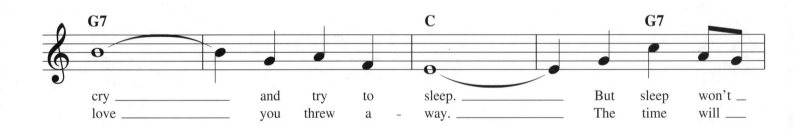

cry _____ and   try   to   sleep. _____ But   sleep   won't _
love _____ you   threw   a - way. _____ The   time   will ____

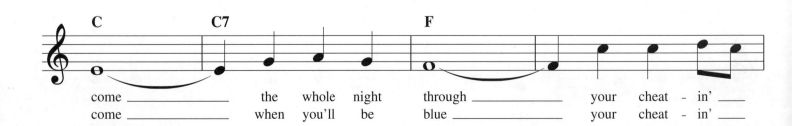

come _____ the   whole   night   through _____ your   cheat - in' ____
come _____ when   you'll   be   blue _____ your   cheat - in' ____